SKATERS, TREK

DAVID
THANKS FOR ALL
YOUR HELP.

D.

SKATERS, TREKKIES

&

COOL DUDES

Book One of

'The Divine Cock-up Trilogy'

By Derek Lawrence

FrontList Books

Published by FrontList Books
An imprint of Soft Editions Ltd,
Gullane, East Lothian, Scotland.

ISBN: 1-84350-098-1

ISBN 13: 9781843500988

To my amazing wife and soul mate Tracy, for her endless patience, understanding, and unconditional belief in me, Gabriel and Embram Ferret Frightener.

To Nicola, Michael, Heather, Ricky, and Grant. My kids, and my never ending source of support throughout. Thanks, and let the good times roll!

PART ONE

'REVELATIONS'

CHAPTER ONE

'In the beginning was the word,' ... or so they say, but in our case 'words' would be far more appropriate. So let me take you on an impossible journey. Allow me to take control of your imagination for the duration of this story. (Shades of the *Twilight Zone* TV series, or what, I hear you say.) Walk with me for a while as we pass through a long corridor, its walls decorated with an ever-shifting pattern of coloured mosaic tiles, the floor almost transparent underfoot. Every now and then doors appear at random intervals, opening, inviting, then disappearing, leaving the wall solid once again. Ahead the corridor ends in a pair of magnificent ornate doors, which neither appear nor disappear. They just *are*. (Confused? Well so am I, and I'm writing this. But then again, in Heaven nothing is quite what it seems.) Listen. Can you hear muffled voices? I know you are itching to open the doors. ... Go on, I dare you ...

"Well, I'm sorry, but I have no idea, OK! None at all! Zero thoughts on the matter! For all I know, he could be stuck in the celestial lift again, or out planning the next judgement day or some other weekend excursion. On the other hand, he could be out creating another universe or two: you know how he loves all that 'And God made the Heavens and the Earth in seven days' stuff! If the truth be known, you're as wise as I am, winged wonder! Who knows what he gets up to these days? Ever since he discovered *Star Trek* he just boldly goes and then boldly comes back again. And did you know he now likes to be known as 'Captain James T.' in certain circles? I'm even informed, by several very reliable sources, that he's taken to wearing the uniform when no one's looking!"

The singsong, Americanised voice of the cherub (whose chosen name was Marcus Enderholt the Third, or Randy to his friends) echoed around the Infinite Hall of Wisdom, its sweet, musical tones turning the polished marble floor into a honey-like liquid, the angelic house guards in their golden armour sighing as they became stuck fast in the sticky mess.

"In any case, aren't you his right hand man? Maybe you should go look for him yourself!"

Gabriel, Archangel on High, Slayer of Demons, First of the Chosen, Member of the Eighth Order of the Nine Ranks of Heavenly Beings, and paint ball champion for the 16th successive millennium, stared at the small child-like figure sitting on the *Steps of Eternity* in front of him. A heavy but well balanced sword of burnished bronze rested on his broad armoured shoulders. He had asked over and over again for an M16 assault rifle, only to be continually told that it *had* to be the infamous *Sword of Retribution*. It was expected by the faithful, he was told. He had no problem with tradition: it was the trappings that went with it that bored him!

"Anyway," the curly-haired boy continued, not pausing for a breath he didn't have to take, seeing as he had no need to breathe in the first place. "In the truest sense of the word, he's not actually lost. After all, how can God get lost? It just isn't possible, is it? To be lost he would have to have been in one specific place to begin with, and as God is omnipresent, it's just not possible, is..." The burnished bronze sword stopped the cherub mid-sentence, its broad tip entering his mouth and exiting through the back of his neck, just around the place where the blonde curls ended and the top set of wing roots began.

"Shut up, will you? Just shut up!" Gabriel's voice exploded around the Art Deco furnished hall, the angelic guards frowning as the liquid they were still stuck in solidified around them. It had been, all in all, a bad day, and even an Archangel had limits to which his patience could be stretched. "Just exactly why he decided to promote you to the rank of High Cherubim is beyond us all! Let alone make you 'Exulted Keeper of the *One's* Whereabouts'. Now tell me Sandy, Mandy or whatever you call yourself these days, where is he?"

As the nearest of the angelic guards crumbled to dust under the onslaught of the Archangel's anger and frustration, Marcus Enderholt (Randy, Mandy, and so on) carefully stood up, the sword pulling out of his head as he backed up the golden steps and away from the perpetrator of such an unnecessarily violent act. Flexing his small wings and reaching up to rub his unmarked neck, the child-like being glared at the tall angel standing not six feet away, his small green eyes narrowing as he slowly walked past Gabriel and up to a small chrome desk which had suddenly appeared out of the marble floor.

"One millennium soon you and the rest of your precious winged army are going to be sorry you didn't treat us with the respect we deserve!" he said furiously. "We have rights you know! Under paragraph 3, section 204a of the *Heavenly Hosts Act*, it clearly states that ..."

"For pity's sake will you just shut up? Right now!" A second angelic guard resigned himself to his inevitable fate, and waited for the Archangel's shout to dissolve him from the inside out. His wait was a short one. "Shut up! Shut up! Shut up!" The shouts now turning to screams of frustration, the remaining guards imploding one by one under the verbal assault. "Will you shut up, you pompous little intestinal worm? Shut up before I ..."

Now many unusual and strange scenes have been witnessed in and around the celestial offices over time immemorial; some, it must be said, far more memorable than others. For example, take the time Lucifer attempted to make Hell a registered charity in order to avoid the Dark Committee's new heating tax; or the day Moses had to explain why he had engraved 'Thou shalt not covet thy neighbour's Marijuana plants' as the eleventh commandment. But a fully-armoured Archangel, High General of the Heavenly Army and 'he who stands at the right hand of the *One*', stamping his feet and screaming like some spoilt child definitely comes high on the list of never to be forgotten sights.

The child-like cherub (who was in fact older than time itself, but had aged quite well considering the stress he had been under recently) sat down in the matching chair which had appeared next to the desk, and revelled in the performance he was being party to. After all, it wasn't every day that the General of the Winged Army lost the plot. Neither was it a common occurrence to see an angel, especially one of this rank and status, babble and rave like some demented demon that had just discovered that his sister had taken Holy Orders.

Now if he had left it there and allowed the situation to resolve itself naturally, tempers would have calmed and pride would have been restored; but no, not this cherub. As usual the last word had to be his, and with any other angel that would have been fine; but when dealing with the right-hand man of the Omnipotent One, caution should always come before confidence. It was at this point that his luck decided to run away screaming.

"Come, come now, Gabe, my good angel! There is no reason for us to fall out over this, is there?" he said condescendingly, milking the few minutes of pleasure for all they were worth. "Tell you what: why not leave it with me, Gabriel, and I will see what I can find out. I'm sure he will turn up at some point: after all, it's getting near to Easter, and you know how much he loves those little cream-filled eggs he insists on having each year."

Picture the scene in greater detail. On the one hand there is Marcus Enderholt the Third (etc., etc., etc.), small, chubby, ageless, blonde and head of the largest union in Heaven; on the other is Gabriel, Archangel, tall, good-looking, angry, and with a very big sword! As a general rule, theologians would probably put forward the argument that angels are perfect beings, lacking the innumerable vices that we mere mortals are plagued with, and are blessed with an inability to do anything which lacks grace, virtue or piety. Well that may be the case with most members of the heavenly multitude, but unfortunately for Marcus (you know the rest), Archangel Gabriel was not only a firm believer in the power of the sword over the pen, he was also very much the exception to most known, and unknown, rules.

The first the cherub knew of the enforced separation was when his head met the marbled floor, bounced twice, and landed face-up at the feet of the furious Archangel.

"Now there was no need for that, was there?" Marcus Enderholt's voice wavered slightly as he realised just how far the Archangel had gone. "I'm sure we can come to some amicable agreement, so just join me back together and we can sit down and talk this whole thing over properly."

Sheathing the sword, Gabriel contemplated for a brief moment just how far into infinity he could kick the talking head, or if he could just lose it somewhere dark and damp for a millennium or two. However, no matter how much he disliked the pompous cherub, one unfortunate and unarguable fact remained: the Omni-One was definitely missing. And that in itself was a first.

Reaching down and picking up the complaining head, Gabriel smiled and dropped it into a dark place for safe keeping.

CHAPTER TWO

Imagine a very large room with floors of polished oak, walls hung with colourful tapestries and furnished in a rich mixture of countless contemporary styles. A board-room, a meeting place and a hive of activity where major business decisions are made. Envisage, if you will, a long table in the centre of this room, lined with leather-bound chairs that are occupied by powerful men making world-altering decisions.

Do you have that picture in your mind? OK, now forget it! Wipe it from your memory and pretend I never mentioned it in the first place. Instead, picture a small cluttered office within an office. Six plastic chairs pulled up around a drop-leaf kitchen table, cold coffee in white polystyrene cups, and a group of unshaven men, all nearer to heart attacks and nervous breakdowns than solving any problems.

Have you pictured that scene instead? OK, forget that as well. In place of it, erase and rewind to another part of your imagination and consider this ...

Gabriel leaned back in the plush synthetic leather chair, the soft material moulding around him as he shifted this way and that in a vague attempt to allow his wings to settle into a more comfortable position. Silently cursing as the sword got in the way (as it always did when he tried to sit down), he finally gave up and resigned himself to losing a few more feathers. Removing the heavy, winged helmet he looked around the wood-panelled office for a few moments, and compared it to his own smaller, but no less impressive, working space. Lifting his sandalled feet, he allowed them to rest on the edge of the huge pine desk. (Just why the Omnificent One liked pine had been a mystery to the Archangel for eons: it was, after all, such a Scandinavian type of wood, and he himself disliked Norway, especially its bloody fjords!) He stared at the signed photograph of the *Enterprise* crew (original series of course, with a special note of thanks from William Shatner) hanging on the wall next to the door, and tried to gather his thoughts.

"Three small questions to answer initially," he said out loud, still not sure if he should even be in this office, let alone sitting in the Omni-One's chair. For this was the place of places, the room where worlds were made and universes sold. It was the very hub of the Omni-One's eternal empire, the special room where he kept his collection of *Star Trek* videos, and the only area of Heaven where you could get a decent cup of real coffee.

"Question number one is 'where?' Number two is 'why?' "

Gabriel paused from his thoughts as he switched on the chrome peculator sitting on a shelf next to the desk, smiling as the fresh aroma of Bolivian coffee started to fill the room.

"And to complete this trio of questions, what happens now?"

Closing his eyes as the smell of the percolating coffee stimulated his nasal senses, the Archangel pondered for a while on the increasing severity of the unfolding problem. The *One* was missing. The *One* was gone. What if he didn't return? What if a power vacuum ensued? For a very brief moment an un-angelic thought of total supremacy crossed his mind ... and then uncrossed it again.

16

The line of souls, saints and other members of the multitude stretched from the office door down Jehovah Way, on to the Well of Souls, passed the Garden of Infinite Grace, turned left at the statue of Saint Kirk (don't ask!) and ended at the two large wooden gates inscribed 'Welcome'. (You didn't really believe the propaganda concerning a certain set of Pearly Gates, did you?) Spaced at regular intervals along its length, soldiers of the *Imperial Angelic Guards Division,* resplendent in their gold-plated armour, stood around wondering just why such a queue existed, let alone why they should be guarding it. Amongst their exalted ranks walked others equally unsure, and just as bewildered. Officers in brilliant silver chain-mail, their immaculately groomed wings shimmering in the celestial light, tried their best to look all-seeing and all-knowing: but, as we all know, appearances can sometimes be deceptive!

"Maybe it's a ticket queue for a new Cliff Richard farewell tour?" The shorter of the two mail-clad angels standing near the front of the line spoke in a whisper, his head bent towards his colleague just in case he might be overheard. "Then again, it's not Boxing Day is it?"

The taller angel looked at his fellow officer, his emotionless face suddenly becoming a picture of puzzlement, tinged with concern.

"Boxing Day? What are you babbling about Boxing Day? Have you been at that funny smelling tobacco again? You know what happened the last time you tried it!"

Asmodel, High Major in the *Fifth Demon Slayers* battalion (the shorter angel to you and I), pointed at the growing queue with his staff of light. "The Boxing Day sales! If today is the day after the day we must all celebrate the arrival of the *One's* nipper, then the sales start today, don't they?"

Abdial (Mr. Taller Angel), also a High Major in that particular branch of the Heavenly Army, forced back a brief smile and shook his head slowly. "Never mind Asmodel, my old friend, I'm sure we can arrange for you to take an extended leave for an eon or two. Maybe you should find yourself a hobby or an outside interest? I'm told that this new wingless sky-diving craze is really taking off among the younger angels. OK, I know they've had a slight problem with something called 'fatal velocity syndrome' of late, but an angel with your flying experience should have no problem coping with a little free-fall turbulence."

Placing an arm around the shoulders of his friend, Abdial started to lead him away from the others, continuing to give words of encouragement, while also preparing to call the Seraphims in white coats as soon as possible.

Gabriel had just finished his second cup of Bolivian coffee when someone knocked on the door. His eyes remained closed as he sat savouring the smooth, silky taste that still ran a marathon around his mouth.

"Better see who that is."

The disjointed voice came from a silk bag hanging from the angel's belt, the words jolting him back from a day-dream trip to Cuba; thoughts of dusky maidens rolling Havana cigars between smooth thighs disappearing far too quickly as reality raised its ugly head yet again. Sitting up in the chair and placing the empty cup next to the still-steaming percolator, the Archangel took the bag from his belt, opened it, and emptied the contents onto the table in front of him.

"Thank you! It's about time, too! What have you carried in that bag recently? It smells worse than one of Lucifer's fart demons!"

The head of Marcus Enderholt the Third (yawn ...) looked up at Gabriel from its temporary resting place on the desk, the small eyes watching intently as the angel once again leaned back into the welcoming softness of the chair.

"Hasn't this gone just a little bit too far, Gabriel? Just reunite me with my other parts and no more will be said about the matter!"

Again the sound of someone knocking on the office door echoed around the room.

"Come on Gabriel, enough is enough! Paragraph 62, sub-section 4 of the *Health and Safety Act* states quite clearly that ..."

It can be very difficult, if not impossible, to talk with your mouth full of Bolivian coffee beans, especially if your mouth is also being held shut by an Archangel with an attitude. Leaning forward, his face only inches away from the head, Gabriel spoke quietly and slowly.

"Listen to me, you insignificant little winged insect! I have an acquaintance who works in a very hot and smelly place, not far from a sign which reads 'Abandon hope all ye who enter here'. This friend owes me a rather large favour; in fact he owes me quite a few, so unless you fancy an eternity as a nodding cherub in the back of Lucifer's private limousine, I suggest you shut up now!"

Again someone knocked on the office door.

"You and I find ourselves in an unfortunate situation; a double-edged sword, so to speak!" continued the Archangel, as Marcus Enderholt's eyes stared at the sheathed sword and then back at the angel. Spitting out the beans and thinking how lucky he was that Indian tea was his preferred drink, the head of the cherub spoke again.

"So exactly what is it you want from me, Gabriel?"

"I want one thing, and one thing only at this particular moment," answered Gabriel. "And that is for you to just listen and try to contemplate the unique set of circumstances we seem to be faced with!"

Resigning himself to his temporary fate the body-less head of the Heavenly Cherubim, Marcus Enderholt the Third (who really cares about the rest?) listened and plotted revenge.

The door was knocked for a fourth time.

CHAPTER THREE

Number 23, Rosewood Drive is situated in a quiet suburb, only three miles from the *Gates of Everlasting Doom,* and five miles from the *Painful Pit of Purgatory.* Its black and white walls, thatched roof and wooden beams show a mock Tudor heritage, and the herb garden is the envy of every witch in the Nine Rings of Hell. If you were to look through one of the small leaded windows or open the carved oak door your view of the interior would be one of elegance and style, with Georgian affluence, Victorian grandeur, and enough darts trophies to shame the fattest of pub players. A home from home and a much needed retreat from the hustle and bustle of life, or in this case death. A house to call one's own, and a place of relaxation when retirement eventually arrives.

Who lives in this picture of idyllic comfort I hear you asking? No one lives here, because number 23, Rosewood Drive is a point of arrival; a collection area for this particular section of Hades, and an oasis of semi-normality within an everlasting nightmare. It is the first port of call for all those who have decided, for one reason or another, that a 'harp and wings' existence is not the afterlife for them. (Well, to be totally accurate, it's now mostly a 'skateboard and iPod' afterlife. Such, I am afraid, is the eternal price of progress!) So, now that specific question has been answered, it's time to move on.

I'm sure you will agree that imagination is a

wonderful thing, but just how good is yours? Walk with me through the oak door, and marvel at its intricate carvings. Admire the ornate brass door-knocker (sorry about its resemblance to a certain impossible position described in the *Kama Sutra*) and delight in the smell of freshly-cut flowers as you enter the brightly lit interior.

OK so far? Very well, let's continue ...

In one corner of this richly decorated room stands a regency table; and behind it a slightly damaged red plastic chair, reminiscent of a time when flared trousers, Space Hoppers, and ABBA were seen as the embodiment of cool.

Slumped in the confines of this piece of 1970's fashion furniture, his tattered, black leather wings crushed and bent against the back of the chair, sits Master Embram Ferret Frightener, gargoyle in charge of arrivals, and lover of small dogs.

Now as far as gargoyles go (and believe me, you would want them to go as far from you as possible), Embram is just about normal for a level 12 demon from the *Chasm of Endless Torment*. Standing at (or in his case, stooping at) a little over 2.5 metres in height, and weighing slightly more than 250kg (OK! so it's a strong chair!), Ferret Frightener has a face reminiscent of a bad tempered Komodo dragon on a Monday morning, and a set of teeth that would make a Nile alligator cry with envy.

But remember, I did say 'just about normal,' didn't I?

On the whole gargoyles have the same sadistic nature as most of the underworld's workers: a prerequisite for any demon. Take, for example, wraiths of doom. Now they love to torment a soul from a distance, moaning and screaming until the unfortunate spirit finally implodes, only to reappear and be tormented over and over again. Or Haborym the Fire Demon and his wife Doris, whose home-made soul candles have always taken pride of place at the annual

Hades Craft Fair. Gargoyles are no exception, enjoying nothing better than removing parts other demons cannot reach. They excel in the finer art of spiritual disembowelment, a skill which calls not only for a total lack of compassion for anything short of their own mother (and even that's questionable), but also requires a keen knowledge of eternal pain and damnation—traits that have made them the most sought-after tormentors in all the pits of Hell, and associated nasty places.

Well all except Embram, that is. So what makes Ferret Frightener unusual, and why do we find him in such a lowly position within the workforce of this foreboding place?

The answer to this perplexing question is two-fold. Firstly, as a gargoyle, Embram suffers from a work-related problem, namely arsonphobia (a fear of fire, for the uninitiated, and something which would obviously inhibit any form of job satisfaction in Hell). Secondly, if you can just use your imagination a little more, you will be able to spot the other part of the answer sleeping on the table next to the Victorian ink pot, and just to the left of the framed photo of Attila the Hun in drag.

To be fair, it's not actually against the rules to have pets in Hell. As a matter of fact, it's rumoured that a certain fallen angel has a tropical fish collection second to none. So what's the problem, I hear you asking? Well, most types of creature are acceptable as a pet or a companion; after all, even demons get lonely sometimes. But a miniature blue-rinse poodle named Fifi Lamoure?

Now humans have the impression that stress is a problem unique to them, and that tension is a homo-sapien related experience handed down through their DNA. Wrong, and wrong again!

"The answer is still no, and no will still mean no the next time you ask!" Embram Ferret Frightener rubbed his brow ridges, trying very hard to ignore the headache imp drilling for oil in his head. Picking up the sheet of parchment, he read it again, trying hard to ignore the continuous barrage of questions being fired at him by the crowd of people that was gathering in increasing numbers in front of the table. But he failed miserably.

He had received the memo at the start of his shift, its orders clear but, none the less, totally mystifying.

'BY ORDER OF THE DARK COUNCIL
'To all intake officers and associated personnel.
'AN IMPORTANT NOTICE.
'As from Torment hour today, all intake and collection stations within the boundaries of the Upper Sub-Levels of The Underworld plc will close until further notice.
'Please ensure that gates are locked and lights turned off.'

He had worked for the Hades Arrivals Department ever since the day his mother discovered his cross-dressing habits and threw him out of the nest. (Understandable, I suppose, if you put yourself in her place. Imagine arriving home to find your foul demon-spawn dressed in a pair of clip-on angel wings, singing *Ave Maria* in a falsetto voice!) As jobs go it was better than most, but worse than some, with few perks and even less in the way of a decent company pension scheme.

On the plus side, though (and that's got to be a bonus in any job in Hell), his direct superior Mr. Ebenezer Polyphemus, Cyclops in Charge (and part-time optician), turned a blind eye to Fifi Lamoure. Not necessarily an unselfish act on his part, but one brought about by chance, circumstances, and a discovered compulsion for artificial flower arranging.

Embram Ferret Frightener gently picked up the sleeping blue-rinse canine from its place of slumber and stroked its soft fur with a well-manicured clawed hand.

24

"Will you all please listen to me?" he said, the words slurring slightly, due to the way his forked tongue flicked in and out as he spoke. "I wish to announce that as from now this arrival point is closed until further notice. Thank you for your patience, and please feel free to recommend us to your family and friends."

If he could count (which was unnecessary in his line of work, mainly due to the fact that anyone finding themselves in this queue was here for eternity anyway), his calculations would have passed 100,000 doomed souls long before he had reached the back door (remember the Tardis?). As the endless line started to disperse, the gathering of the damned heading back out of the door and on to the upwards escalator, Ferret Frightener closed his intake register and stood waiting for the room to finally clear.

But, as usual, nothing was going to be that easy...

"No! It's not good enough! I will not be treated like this!" Above the hum of the air conditioners and the distant sound of the bone grinding factory which had just started the morning shift, a shrill, piercing voice assaulted the delicate linings of his pointed ears.

"Do you know who I am? I demand to see someone or something in charge!"

In every crowd there is always one. Someone who thinks the universe owes him a place in the grand order of things; a nobody living in a private world of delusion. A private imaginary place where he or she believes they are better than everyone else. Yes, there is always one, and this crowd was no exception.

Gently placing the waking poodle back down on the desk, the gargoyle made a mental note not to forget the lights, and waited.

He didn't have to wait long.

Pushing his way through the multitude of confused and terrified souls, whose eternity of pain and damnation had been postponed for at least today, came one

Eric Wainright Smythe, of the Sussex Smythes. Resplendent in a designer label double-breasted suit (in blue stretched wool, with jetted lapels), the short, fat, balding fifty two year old stockbroker (well, recently deceased stockbroker to be precise) forced his way forward.

Fifi Lamoure scratched at the pink, diamond-studded collar and silently passed wind (a creature like Fifi would never do anything as crude as fart), her breeding and finesse fighting back the urge she had to clean areas of her body she refused to believe existed. Stretching out on the smooth, polished wood, the blue-rinse poodle ignored the approaching man, even when his two fists met the table in front of her.

"Who are you? And where is He?" Spittle flew from the fat man's mouth as he shouted at Embram, droplets falling on the immaculately groomed fur of Miss Lamoure. "I demand that he is here to welcome me! Him or his son! So, you ugly creature, slither away and fetch them now!"

As all dedicated students of the dark arts should know, gargoyles are not noted for their sense of humour. Nor do they take kindly to being compared to a snake, or any other creature that moves about via belly motion (that aside, Embram just hated the gross way that they shed their skins). Without moving from his position in the plastic chair, Ferret Frightener nodded his head slightly before speaking, a smile trying in vain to form on his uneven lips.

"I see. So just who is it you wish to have here to greet you on your arrival, may I ask?"

"Him, damn you! Big G or JC!" shouted Mr. Fat, still spraying spittle as he continued to rant and rave. "Or even both of them! Like I told Mr. Grim Reaper when he knocked on my boardroom door this morning, I expect nothing else but the best even if I am deceased!"

"Actually, it was last Monday," interrupted Embram,

the smile still losing its battle with his lips. "The Angel of Death came for you a week ago today, Mr. Smythe." Pausing for a moment, the gargoyle opened his register and glanced at the page. "It seems that you have been held up in transit, due to a staff shortage at Hell's Gate Number 4."

"Sorry? What are you talking about?" Mr. 'Spray-my-spittle' had suddenly lost the urge to shout, his dead brain struggling to dismiss what his dead ears were hearing. "Hell's Gate? What do you mean Hell's Gate?"

In retrospect, I take back the bit about gargoyles not having a sense of humour. As the smile finally won its battle against eons of demon evolution, Embram Ferret Frightener delivered the Coup de Grace, an act now being witnessed by those temporarily reprieved souls who had halted their departure from the room.

"Very well, Mr. Spit, for Hell's Gate may I suggest you read 'the gateway to Hell'? It's quite simple really," he was enjoying this, and it showed. "This, my dear Mr. Spittle, is the end of the road, so to speak; the final part of your journey from there to here, and the conclusion of a wasted and selfish life. This, Mr. Mighty-Mouth Smythe, is where your sanity leaves for an extended holiday, and an eternity of pain and very nasty things begins!"

It took the soul-brain of Eric Wainright Smythe (late of the Sussex Smythes) one third of no time at all to comprehend the everlasting implication of the message it was receiving.

"No! No! I'm sure there's been some mistake!" Panic kicked him between his spirit legs as he started to back away from the table, heading towards the door as he reversed his way through the onlooking crowd. "I think I might just go and maybe try somewhere else, if that's all right with you?"

Mistake number one!

It happens occasionally (well, quite often actually. In

fact, to tell the truth, every day on a very large scale) that newly arrived souls decide that an eternity spent in torment, damnation and pain is not really to their liking. An understandable sentiment when you consider just what damnation entails. On a good day Embram would simply eat them and regurgitate them later, making up the excuse that it was all part of the overall plan. Or he would call the clean-up imps, whose methods and ethics were questionable, even in Hell.

Well, today he was regretting even getting up. His horns hurt, his wings felt as if they were encased in ice and the headache imp was now trying to remove his eyes from the inside. Not a good day for anyone to rub his scales the wrong way. Leaning forward in the chair, Ferret Frightener whispered to the poodle and returned to his original position, the smile on his face growing larger.

Eric Wainright Smythe, of the Sussex Smythes, stopped backing away as Fifi Lamoure jumped down from the table and walked up to him.

"So, you're not happy with what we have on offer, Mr. Smythe?" Embram allowed a little steam to escape from his flared nostrils, a trick that always went down well at dinner parties (but boy did it hurt the sinuses). "Well we can't have that now, can we? What do you think we should do for the gentleman, Fifi?"

Sitting down directly in front of the puzzled soul, her head tilted to one side, the blue-rinse poodle dropped the ball which had suddenly appeared in her mouth.

"Oh, so you want to play, do you?" said the gargoyle. "Please, Mr. Smythe, indulge her while I think about what the best strategy is for us all."

Suddenly relieved that things were not as bad as they first seemed, Wainright Smythe bent down to pick up the ball.

Mistake number two!

She could have simply just got on with it, but like everything else Fifi Lamoure did, it had to be done in style. The change was instantaneous; even Embram had difficulty keeping up with the metamorphic process, but then again he had difficulty doing just about anything today.

They still talk about it in the bars in Hell even now. Pay a visit to the *Sultry Soul* wine bar on a Friday night and someone, or something, will mention the dog thief Hercules. (OK, OK, I know it was one of his twelve labours, and I suppose the real blame should be directed at King Eurystheus himself. But that's showbiz, as they say ... They don't? Well they should!) Not a popular hero in the dark lands is our Hercules: not a popular hero at all! To kill the Hydra was one thing: after all, who was going to miss a nine-headed serpent with chronic halitosis and ringworm? And let's face it, who really cares how many golden apples he pinched? Zeus had gone off cider at the time anyway. No, it was the twelfth labour that finally went beyond the boundaries of accepted behaviour. Dog-napping Cerberus put Hercules on the wrong side of Mr. Fallen Angel's fifth wife Persephone; a very homely woman who had always planned to show Cerberus at Crufts one day.

But remember, not all tales told in bars are quite what they seem.

A soul has no need for bodily functions, nor does it have to fear embarrassing moments such as breaking wind in a public place, or being caught in a fast food restaurant over the age of eighteen. The soul of Eric Wainright Smythe was a little different. It didn't like hamburgers ... but it did wet itself.

Looking up from his stooped position, the ball he had just picked up falling from his shaking hand, Eric

Wainright Smythe didn't feel the warm trickle of liquid running down his leg, or notice that his non-existent bowels had suddenly discovered a will of their own. His sanity had travelled far, far away, while his spirit mind concentrated on something much more important. Fifi Lamoure was gone. In her place stood his own personal apocalypse, a 400 kilogram mass of teeth, saliva and attitude. Something that watched him through six glowing eyes as his own glazed over.

It was the middle head that caught him, the left one that began the digestive process and the right one that ended it. Breakfast, dinner and tea, all combined in one single, fresh soul meal. Much better than dog biscuits, and far more entertaining than a rubber ball!

Belching gas that could dissolve titanium at three miles, Cerberus licked his three pairs of lips, farted twice, and turned away from the puddle of ectoplasm that had once been Smythe of the Sussex Smythes.

As Embram Ferret Frightener let the smile win once again, Cerberus changed back into Fifi Lamoure, jumped up into his lap, rubbed against the scaled skin of his broad chest and settled down to sleep. Gently stroking the poodle as it dozed, Embram watched the last of the reprieved souls leave the room, the increasing pain in his head confirming the arrival of yet another headache imp.

Contemplating a warm shower, lunch and the rest of the day in bed, the gargoyle picked up his register and headed homewards, his mental note about the lights falling over itself in a vain attempt to be remembered.

He had just reached the door when the phone rang.

CHAPTER FOUR

Throughout his divine existence as an Archangel Gabriel had faced one crisis after another, not with an air of celestial grace and fortitude, but with an attitude that dictated, 'if you can't solve the problem right away, then take it out on someone else.' A philosophy that had served him well until now, and still did.

He thought 'candle, times three,' and they appeared. Thin ones I grant you, but candles all the same.

"This is going to hurt, I know, but understand it is an act born out of necessity. It's better that no one actually sees us together until we find out what's happening, so just grin and bear it. The sooner I find out what the situation is, the sooner I can re-unite you with your other half." (Not quite the full facts, as the body of Marcus Enderholt had in truth gone walkabout, searching no doubt for its missing portion.) "Why not look upon it as a career change? One that takes you from humble shop steward to temporary new-age candle holder."

Gabriel turned the head of the cherub to one side as he continued the inane chatter. "It has to be better than calling a strike every time there's a dispute over some petty breach of regulations, surely?" Pushing a red, tapered candle into an ear, and then turning the protesting head to repeat the process on the other side, he ignored the understandable increase in verbal abuse streaming from the open mouth, and picked up the third.

"What ... what are you doing?" screamed Marcus Enderholt. "I'll have you for this! You wait and see! You're finished, you winged bastard! Do you hear me, finished!"

The onslaught of insults was abruptly terminated when the last candle found its mark, the cherub's eyes bulging as the Archangel forced the wax object deeper into the mouth than was really necessary.

"Just think yourself lucky I'm in a good mood!" Gabriel said with a smile. "I could easily have made them church candles."

As the door was knocked for the fifth time, the angel thought 'let there be light,' and nodded with satisfaction as the three candles flickered into life.

"It's just like Christmas! Perhaps we could arrange a new annual job for you and your fellow socialites. 'Cherubim Candle Hire,' maybe, or how about 'Enderholt's Novelty Wax Sculptures,' ... Just think!" The smile grew broader as Gabriel moved towards the door. "With my help, you could 'get a head' of the opposition!"

With the smell of the melting wax filling his nostrils and his eyes streaming with tears of rage, frustration and smoke inhalation, Marcus Enderholt the Third (Mandy, Dandy, Andy, or whatever: you decide which one) continued to plan his revenge.

Looking out over the head of the figure standing in the now open doorway, Gabriel's face took on an air of confusion for a brief moment as his eyes scanned the endless queue stretching onwards into infinity.

"What in heaven?" he said, to no one in particular. "Is Cliff Richard touring again?"

It was a feminine voice that brought his attention back to the person who had been responsible for the knocking.

"Hello Mr. Archangel ... I'm down here! HELLO!"

Writing a mental memo to collect his allotted concert

ticket from the box office (it was a pity Alice Cooper wasn't touring this millennium, but a free ticket *is* a free ticket after all) Gabriel forced his gaze away, stepped back, and looked down in the direction of the voice.

"Archangel Gabriel? High General of the Heavenly Army, Slayer of all Foul Creatures from the Six Pits of Damnation, and he who sits with pride within the hallowed hall of eternity?"

"Yes! Yes! I am he, and yes I'm all of the other grand titles you are about to use. Who are you? And what is it you want, I'm very busy!" (Actually, he was becoming a little concerned about the smell of burning from the room behind him. As you can imagine, in Heaven arson is always taken very seriously.)

Standing a good half a metre shorter than the angel, her ample frame only just harnessed within a suit of gold Kevlar armour (progress once again, I'm afraid), stood Brynhildr Nielsen, employee of the Valkyrie Messenger Service.

"So, Miss Nielsen, what can I do for you?" Quickly looking back into the room as he spoke, he was relieved to see it was still intact.

"Wow! They were right! They said you were brilliant, but that was amazing! How do you do it?"

"Sorry?"

"My name? How did you know my name? The other girls said you were good, but that was unbelievable!"

Gabriel sighed. "Why oh why did they ever agree to keep on employing the Valkyrie after the Norse Gods went into bankruptcy?" he thought to himself. "Your badge," he said, pointing at the plastic tag attached to the breast plate. "Your name is printed on your badge!"

If there is one thing more annoying than lice in your wing feathers, it's a Valkyrie with a fit of the giggles. Flushed with embarrassment (and with a little hero worship thrown in), Brynhildr Nielsen cleared her throat, unrolled the papyrus scroll she carried, and began to deliver the message.

"By order of the Celestial High Council, it is decreed that Archangel Gabriel, High General of the Heavenly Army, Slayer of All Foul Creatures from the Six Pits of Damnation, He who sits with pride ..."

What little patience he had was wearing thin as he resisted the urge to add a second head to his collection.

"We've already gone through all of that! Will you just get on and deliver the message please?"

"From the beginning?" she said.

"No! Just skip the titles and get to the point!"

Drumming his fingers lightly on the hilt of his sword, Gabriel considered how the Valkyrie and the cherub would look together, as night lights on his bedside table.

"By order of the high council ... Oh, sorry, I've done that bit, haven't I?"

His fingers gripped the sword hilt tightly. 'Soon,' he thought, 'very soon, if she keeps this up!'

"By order of ... etc., etc., etc. Oh! I'm so sorry about this Mr. Gabriel!" she said, as alarm started to take up residence in her mind. "Just a moment, let me just find where the main message starts ... Ah yes, here we are ..."

Brushing back her blonde hair, Brynhildr blushed slightly as she shuffled from one foot to the other. This was her first assignment, and it wasn't going well. Not at all well. Wetting her dry lips with the tip of her tongue, she started to read again. "... should hereby take notice that his prompt attendance is required at an emergency contingency meeting, to be held within the Chapter House of Committee Block Three at five past Vespers today. Light refreshments and confession will be supplied."

Rolling up the parchment and handing it to him,

Valkyrie Brynhildr Nielsen, of the aforementioned messenger service, waited to be dismissed.

"I suppose you're waiting for a tip?" Gabriel said, taking the scroll. "Well I don't usually tip lower orders, but in your case I'll make an exception. Get a larger suit of armour or lose weight!"

Ignoring the sudden flood of tears brought on by his not so generous words of encouragement, Gabriel turned and was about to re-enter the room, when something pulling on the hem of his cloak stopped him.

"Oh for pity sake, what now!" He was starting to get very irritated indeed.

"Mr. Gabriel, do you have a minute, sir?"

Spinning round on his heels the angel almost tripped over the small, bald oriental gentleman in saffron robes standing to one side of the door.

"Yes?" he said abruptly. "Don't tell me! I bet you have a message for me as well!"

"A message? No, sorry sir, should I have?"

A vivid picture of a small, bald, three stick Buddhist incense holder suddenly appeared in his head as he struggled to keep control of his temper.

"Never mind, just what is it you want?"

"My name is Doryu Lee." (Which when translated from its native tongue, means 'Way of the Dragon'. I'll leave you to guess his Earthly name ... Bruce.) "I am Intake Supervisor, First Class, responsible for processing all arrivals, and ensuring their smooth transition into the afterlife."

Gabriel was getting bored.

"Yes, I know who you are, Mr. Lee. Indirectly you work for me, so what is it you actually want?"

"Then you will also know, sir, that I am the official representative of the *Intake and Spiritual Readjustment Union,* and my members are demanding a managerial explanation."

Contemplating the finer things in the hereafter is something angels do in their spare time; they also pride themselves on their inherent tolerance and understanding. All angels, that is, but one.

"What explanation would you like?" Boredom was turning to aggression. "How about I explain just how much I hate certain aspects of my job, for a start! Have you any idea what it's like to have such a responsible position within the hierarchy of this place? No, of course you don't, do you? Take last weekend, for example ..."

"Ah yes, that is as may be, sir," the monk interrupted, "but what we really demand to know, sir, is why ..."

He had two chances: slim and none. None won. Ignoring the interruption, the Archangel continued his verbal barrage.

"While you and your saffron-clad friends were off chanting your mantras, or whatever they're called, I was sat in a stuffy office planning our strategy for the next bi-millennial volleyball championship. Did you know the Beelzebub Bullfrogs have won five times in a row? One more victory and they get to keep the 'Head of John the Baptist Trophy'!" Being an angel and thus not having the need to breathe, Gabriel didn't pause for breath. "And take today! You have no idea how much my stress levels have risen, or just how much pressure I'm under. Now, tell me Mr. Lee, do you like candles?"

"Do I like candles? Well yes, I suppose I do, but all of this has no relevance at all to my question, does it?"

A now very irritated Gabriel had just started to draw the sword from its scabbard when he smelt pungent smoke drifting from the room behind him, but it was the panicking voice of Marcus Enderholt the Third (blah! blah! blah!) that finally saved the Buddhist from the Archangel's bad karma.

"OK! OK! What's the question? Come on, I don't have all day!" he said, glancing behind him. "Come on will you, what is it?"

"My members demand to know why all the intake and collection offices have just been closed without any prior consultation. Do you realise how many inductions we were expecting today?"

For a brief moment Gabriel forgot about the worsening smell and tried to ignore the cries for help that were emanating from the room with ever increasing volume.

"Closed? Are you sure? Maybe maintenance crews are carrying out vital repairs, or testing a new alarm system."

"Yes, sir, of course I'm sure they are closed. The shutters went down only moments after the second shift clocked on! This is a clear infringement of the *Single Gate Agreement,* and something my union will be taking very seriously! The wording of the agreement is very clear and precise, and not open to negotiation or change without the prior consent of all parties."

Pacing back and forth, lost in his own minor self-importance, the small, bald figure continued to press home his point long after Gabriel had re-entered the room, closing the door behind him.

"Our problem has just expanded!" said Gabriel, walking towards the table. "It seems the situation has grown to mammoth proportions, and is still growing. It looks as if ... oops!" He stopped dead in his tracks, his eyes widening, his face breaking into a broad smile of self-satisfaction.

"Oops! Is that all you have to say, you flying, armoured freak?" the bald and blackened head of Marcus Enderholt (now Mr. Angry to his friends) screamed at him, a hardening mess of melted wax having long since replaced the three candles. Gabriel slowly walked around the table and sat down.

"That is it! I'll make sure they throw the book at you! No, I'll make sure they throw the whole bloody library!" Enderholt's angry head wobbled slightly as his fury grew in intensity, remnants of burnt hair falling in a small pile on the table. "Assault, that's what it is, assault and flattery!" the head screamed, spraying wax and spittle over the polished wood.

"Battery!" Gabriel said, brushing bits of wax from his face. "It's assault and battery."

"Battery? What are you talking about, battery? I'm going to make you wish you were never created! They will clip your wings and then give you bollocks so they can clip them as well!"

"Dear me! Such language, Mr. Cherub," Gabriel mocked. "I wonder what the Grand Committee of Hosts would say if they heard you utter such blasphemies. In fact, I wonder what the consequences would be if they knew about your Friday night excursions to *Dante's Inferno Bar* in Purgatory. Or maybe your clandestine meetings each month with a certain Succubus lap-dancer and her fork-tongued friend?"

The outpouring of threats ceased, the eyes of the head narrowing in response to the angel's words. When he spoke again, Marcus Enderholt did so in a guarded whisper.

"Just exactly how do you know about any of that, Gabriel? How much do you know?"

"I make it my place to know everything, stupid! Why do you think you are just a worthless cherub, Enderholt, and I am who I am? It may surprise you to also hear that I even know about your little export business."

The head of Marcus Enderholt suddenly wished it could close its eyes and wake up a long way from the desk ... and the Archangel.

"Ingenious, I must admit, and very profitable I would imagine. I'm all for private enterprise and the free market economy; but I ask you, selling clip on angel wings to demons with a taste for the unusual? That, Mr. Enderholt, could cost you your own wings."

The head said nothing as Gabriel picked it up and dropped it back into the bag hanging on his belt.

"That's better. Now I would be grateful if you could remain quiet for a while, we have a meeting to attend and I would prefer to do all the talking."

Walking back out through the door, and ignoring the now irate monk whose voice was slowly getting higher and higher with rage, Gabriel smiled again and patted the bag:

"Oh, and by the way, about your business empire— your new partner will accept the generous cut of 60% which you are, of course, about to offer."

CHAPTER FIVE

The phone call was, in a sense, a virtual reality experience: the ring tone picked up by a computer chip buried deep within his limited imagination. (I know; you're thinking 'a gargoyle with an imagination?' A radical idea maybe, but I did say this one was different, didn't I?)

Embram Ferret Frightener (he had never understood the second part of his name, mainly because he had never even seen a ferret, let alone frightened one) had signed the petition against the introduction of the integrated bio-phone system, along with countless other minor demons. The fear of internal phone bugging was a serious consideration unless you happened to be a certain demon ant-eater named Hardvark Long Tongue, who never quite grasped the fact that internal bugging didn't actually mean a built-in food chain. Every union in the underworld had threatened some form of independent action as a protest, with one actually bringing its members out on strike. Unfortunately, a unilateral walkout by the *Affiliated Union of Molten Rocks* had little effect on the outcome of the proceedings. Hell may be run by a committee these days, but the real power still resides within the walls of the great house. Well, to be accurate, within the walls of the great penthouse. A modest one hundred room residence taking up the top ten floors of the *Angel Falls* apartment complex; small and compact by the Dark One's usual standards, but far easier to maintain. A very important consideration when you take into account the cut in his domestic budget imposed by the Committee of Internal Affairs during a surprise internal audit.

The phone conversation itself was a more or less one-sided affair: nothing extraordinary in that considering the limited social skills of the temps employed by the *Harpies Secretarial Agency*. But it was the message itself which started alarm bells ringing in Embram's head ... his hands, his feet, and other parts of his ample body.

"Am I speaking to Ebamam Ferret Worrier?"

'Why didn't anyone ever get his name right?' he thought to himself.

"The name is actually Embram Ferret Frightener, and yes, I am he."

"I am Miss Popodoxsalis, secretary assigned to the Dark Council Sub Committee for this millennium, and I am calling from the office of 'He who makes all that lives tremble with terror when they look upon his face, the Lord of all foul flying and crawling things, Dark Angel of the underworld, and He who is the destroyer of worlds and all who ..."

At this point Embram fed Fifi, filled in the report sheet for the day's shift, and calculated that he had just about enough time to call his mother before the seemingly endless list of titles ended.

Mother wasn't in.

"... supreme being, above even he who thinks he is so clever and without fault ... which of course we all know he isn't."

The gargoyle stifled a yawn.

"Ebamin Stoat Killer?"

"Whatever!" He was tired and bored by this point, but he had to admit he quite liked 'Stoat Killer.'

"I'm sorry, Mr. Stoat Killer?"

"Yes, that is me! Exactly what is it you want?"

"You are summoned to attend a meeting at *Angel Falls* within an allotted time period. Report to the reception desk on arrival, and please ensure that you are prompt. Oh, and please note that formal dress is expected, Mr. Emgram."

"Formal dress?" thought Embram, as the virtual line in his head went dead. "*Angel Falls?* I'm summoned to *Angel Falls?*"

Personal fear had been unknown to the gargoyle (unless you include the time he tried bungee jumping over *Lava Falls),* but that had now changed. Looking at the sleeping poodle curled up in his lap, Embram's head was suddenly filled with one very unpleasant thought. "For pity's sake," he said, "what if they know all about you?"

If he had been able to grow hairs on the back of his neck, they would be standing up by now. His whole body suddenly became tense with worry as other thoughts flooded his mind.

"What if they know it was me who took you, Fifi, and now they want you back?"

Worry turned into panic, panic made way for fear, and fear ran away when terror said "Hello Embram, I'm your new friend!"

"What if it's actually *HIM* who wants to see me in person?"

Even terror deserted him as Embram realised what such a summons to *Angel Falls* could mean to his future existence. Like every other employee of the dark underworld, he had been brought up on a regular diet of terrible tales, shadowy stories, and unmentionable nightmares. A web of deceit, spun from lies, half truths and devious propaganda. He was scared: scared, terrified and turning to stone inside. But he was also strangely excited at the prospect.

"Me, actually inside *Angel Falls?*" he said to himself (well he was alone after all, unless you counted a sleeping poodle; and even if he hadn't been, no one seemed to listen these days). "Me, summoned to appear before *Him?*" Leaning his head to one side, Embram smiled as he let a pleasant thought creep in. "Maybe I'm due for promotion. Or could it be a surprise dinner for my eons of dedicated service?"

For a brief millisecond in a timeless place, Embram Ferret Frightener (he still quite liked 'Stoat Killer'; but like a ferret, he had no idea what a stoat actually was) embraced hope and gave optimism a very wet and smelly kiss.

The nice thought disappeared, as a 'feed me now!' growl from the blue-rinse poodle on his lap forced the more plausible reason for the summons back into his thought processes.

"No, that's it, I'm finished! It's all over!" The gargoyle looked down at the poodle who was now chewing at his talons; dinner time had passed but her hunger had only increased. "They are going to take you away from me, and bury this poor gargoyle deep in some smelly shite pile for the rest of eternity and beyond." Terror was back now, dancing in his head. "Bury me deep, and forget I was ever hatched!"

Ignoring the small fact that Fifi had chewed off two of his claws, Embram Ferret Frightener cradled the small dog as he stood up and looked around the empty room, before making his way to the exit. Switching off the lights on the way and opening the carved oak door, he stepped out and walked slowly past the herb garden and up to the small wooden gate. Stroking the poodle and looking back towards the cottage, Embram Ferret Frightener sighed and resigned himself to his inevitable, and almost certainly painful, fate. Looking down at Fifi, asleep again in his arms, he squeezed her gently, re-grew the missing claws and wondered just where he could pick up a cheap dinner jacket in his size.

CHAPTER SIX

He arrived at the *Angel Falls* complex early, uncomfortable in the tight-fitting dinner jacket. (His friend Wagstaff Nose Cruncher may have been a classy dresser, but the size difference between a gargoyle and a minor golem is quite noticeable, especially in the chest area.) He was also totally confused about just what the bow tie was actually used for (but he had to admit it looked quite good tied around his head: and red did match the colour of his eyes today). Stepping out of the taxi cab, his bent tail and aching back an indication of the lack of space allocated to passengers of his stature, Embram Ferret Frightener paid the impeccably uniformed Zombie driver and watched as the vehicle shifted dimension and floated off in search of another fare. Turning round, Embram stared upwards, onwards, and into infinity.

Towering above him was the *Angel Falls* apartment complex, its chrome, glass and steel structure stretching up and beyond the bounds of his sight, its vast size momentarily scrambling his visual senses as he gazed in genuine wonder and amazement. The building stood on the corner of *Idi Amin Avenue* and *Pol Pot Road*, the heart of an extensive residential district, and the epicentre of Hell's elite accommodation for its more select denizens. Around the edges of this mini city stood numerous wine bars and infamous night clubs: dens of unbelievable vice and iniquity, establishments of notoriety in an underworld where excess and debauchery are the accepted, and the expected, norms. (Well, that was according to his friend Wagstaff, who visited one of the clubs from time to time, and who had told him that it was the only area in Hell where it was even possible to purchase clip-on angel wings ... *if*, of course, you had the right contacts.) Stretching away in all directions, immaculately clean, tree-lined roads led directly towards the heart of the metropolis, chrome street lamps illuminating the area with a soft, yellow light.

For a brief moment in time (actually, if you think about it, quite a difficult concept to grasp in a place where time doesn't exist) Embram Ferret Frightener let a nice thought fight its way through the trepidation; his mind concentrating on Fifi, who was safely hidden away in a secure place. Just in case.

But then, as fast as it had appeared, it was gone ...

Deep in the pit of his more than generous stomach, twelve legged carnivorous butterflies flew in circles. His whole body tensing, he made his way slowly towards a revolving glass door. Breathing in, he squeezed through and entered a brightly lit foyer, his inner eyelids closing momentarily as the glare from the overhead lights blinded him. As his vision returned, Embram stood and looked around at the spotlessly clean reception area.

Polished chrome and leather chairs stood empty, lined up against teak panelled walls covered in priceless medieval tapestries and pre-Raphaelite art. Beneath his bare feet was a highly polished, pristine, oak floor. The centre of the room was dominated by a large, round mahogany table, most of its surface covered by a brass engraving, its legs immaculately carved and shaped in a mock Georgian style. Above his head hung row after row of Art Deco lamps, their angular shades doing little to disperse the intense light emitted by the tungsten bulbs; and ahead of him, built into the wood panelled wall, stood the reception desk. The desk's rosewood counter was level with the upper chest of the large, brown rabbit standing directly behind it.

"Can I help you at all?" Looking up from whatever it was doing, the creature stared at Embram Ferret Frightener over wire rimmed glasses, its voice emotionless as it made no attempt to hide the look of derision in its eyes.

"You're a rabbit!" Embram blurted out.

"I'm sorry, what did you say?"

"I said 'you're a rabbit'!"

Audibly sighing, the large brown furry thing removed the glasses, leaned forward on the counter, and closed its eyes for a brief moment of contemplation.

"I am, in fact, a hare. Well, to be precise, I'm Dingle Shagbat, familiar, and one time companion, of Miss Hannah Shripmere of Gloucester; presently between engagements and acting as receptionist at this prestigious establishment."

Now as you may have already guessed from previous episodes, it's very rare to see someone smile in Hell, let alone laugh; but not only did the smile return to Embram's lips, it also brought a friend.

"*The* Hannah Shripmere?" The smile increased in size as its friend, the laugh, grew in Embram's chest. "Old Hannah Shripmere, the dyslexic witch who signed her soul over to Santa?" The smile milked the opportunity for all it was worth, the gargoyle's grin growing with each passing second. "The one and only Witchy Shripmere? The only satanic (or was it Santatanic?) servant in the history of infinity to regularly send each new pope a congratulations card on their inauguration?"

Replacing the glasses, Dingle Shagbat (who had always had a burning desire to know just why mistress Shripmere had given him such an odd name. 'Dingle' was OK as far as familiar names went, but 'Shagbat' ... he hated bats!) looked up at the brightly lit ceiling in despair and then back at the gargoyle.

"Look, just what is it I can do for you? I've had a very busy day and it's getting near to my shift change; so if you don't mind, could we please dispense with any more pointless repartee or chitchat and just get to the point?"

Feeling another attack of laughter welling up inside him, and worried about just how much more strain the already stretched dinner jacket could take, Embram Ferret Frightener forced a serious expression on to his face and walked over to the desk.

"I have an appointment."

"Sorry?"

"I said 'I have an appointment'."

Removing the glasses again and polishing the lenses on his fur, Dingle Shagbat replaced them on the end of his twitching nose and opened the large leather-bound book that lay on the desk in front of him.

"*You* have an appointment? So what is the name, may I enquire?"

"What is the name of what?"

"*Your* name, what is *your* name?" His despair growing, Dingle Shagbat prepared himself for more unpaid overtime.

"Ferret Frightener, my name is Embram Ferret Frightener!"

Sighing again and running a well manicured paw down a short list of names, Dingle Shagbat's eyes widened as he came to the ninth one down.

"Oh yes, it seems you do have an appointment, Mr. Ferret Flogger. If you would kindly go to room two: it's the door on your left."

"Thank you, and the name is Embram Ferret *Frightener,* not *'Flogger'!*"

"I'm very sorry, Mr. Flogger, what was that you said?"

"Oh nothing, forget it! Which door did you say?"

Forcing back an overwhelming urge to phone his demon friend Otis Myxomatosis and arrange a surprise party for Dingle Shagbat, Embram opened the door marked 'Appointments' and entered the room.

The door disappeared behind him.

"I take it that you are Everam Weasel Squeezer?" The squeaky voice came from a small, fat, balding man, dressed in an expensive looking black dinner suit and sitting behind a wooden desk in the middle of the otherwise bare room.

"What?"

"Are *you* Everam Weasel Squeezer?"

Usually his patience would have been exhausted by now, his temper bursting forth and urging him to tear the head off the next person, or thing, to get his name wrong. Something he would have done, if it hadn't been for one very important fact of the afterlife.

If this was *Angel Falls*, which he knew it was; and seeing that a certain Lord of all Foulness lived at *Angel Falls*, which he knew he did; then a simple process of deduction led to only one conclusion: was this *Him*?

Looking at the smaller than expected man, Embram suddenly felt a little cheated.

"Well! are you that creature?" The squeaky voice spoke again.

"Am I what creature?"

"Are you Everam Weasel Squeezer? You must be deaf or just very stupid!"

Not sure if he should grovel, bow, remove his own head, or tear apart the obnoxious thing sitting in front of him, Embram decided to ride his bicycle down the safer road of caution, just in case. (It was one of Wagstaff's little sayings, but what in all of Hell's gates a *bicycle* was, he had no idea.)

Bowing as low as he could, his wings involuntarily opening and tearing the jacket in two as they ex-

48

panded, the confused gargoyle stared at the mosaic tiled floor as he spoke.

"I am humbly that creature, oh great Satanic Dark Lord of the Black Pit. I ask that you look favourably upon this, your worthless and corrupt servant (and fully paid up union member), who hath been summoned to kneel before your magnificence. Let this foul spawn bathe within your dark aura, oh mighty and terrible one. Let this servant ..."

The squeaky voice stopped him in mid-sentence.

"Will you shut up and stop grovelling?"

For a moment Embram was unsure what was happening, but before looking up he added, for good measure, "and I would like to make it clear, right now, that I do not own a pet of any kind, especially a dog, specifically a poodle, and particularly one with more than one head."

"What in the Nine Rings of Hell are you babbling on about? What's all this rubbish about a poodle bathing in my dark aura? My name is Simon Sharp, Minister of Internal Affairs on the Dark Council, and Hell's official representative on the joint Darkness & Light Emergency Committee."

For a few brief seconds (before you point out the obvious, I know it's a place where time has no existence, but let's just call it artistic licence, shall we?) a look of puzzlement crossed the man's face, only to be quickly replaced with one of sudden realisation.

"Ah, I see!" He said, grinning broadly. "You think I'm the *main man,* don't you? You are under the understandable assumption that you are in the dark and terrible presence of *Him!*" The grin widened and met at the back of his head. "I suppose I should be flattered, but then again, what more should I have reasonably expected from a thing such as you?"

Removing what was left of Wagstaff's dinner jacket (and hoping that his friend had no functions to attend for the foreseeable future), Embram Ferret Frightener flexed his aching wings and growled deeply. It was embarrassment that now paid him a visit, and, as usual, anger wasn't far behind.

"Are you telling me that I'm *not* here because of Fifi? That I haven't been summoned to say sorry to Mr. Muscles for spoiling one of his pathetic labours?"

Councillor Sharp, in his sharp dinner suit, moved the chair closer to the desk and leaned forward, staring at the gargoyle in disbelief, tinged with boredom.

"Fifi? Just what is a Fifi? And who in Heaven is this Mr. Muscles?" Resting his chin in cupped hands, he looked directly at Embram and sighed deeply. "Listen to me Everam, Ebenezer, or whatever else your pathetic little name may be. I have no idea why they chose a lizard like you for this job, but they have. So shut up and listen to me!"

Embram's eyes narrowed as anger was pushed aside by fury, his talons flexing as he felt his self-control running away.

"Lizard! You called me a lizard! If you weren't one of the dark council I would ..."

"But I *am* a council member, you worthless pile of swamp filth, and you are just something that crawled from a slime pit! You mean nothing to me! Do you understand what I'm saying? You are absolutely, and totally, a nothing to me!"

What happened next not only took Embram by surprise, it also made fury run away to hide, and the headache imp return with its pneumatic drill.

Without seemingly moving, Mr. Sharp suddenly reappeared in front of the startled gargoyle; a row of black, lidless eyes and newly-grown fangs only inches away from Embram's face. The fact that Mr. Sharp had now taken on the appearance of a giant hairy arachnid had a very distinct bearing on Embram's sudden need to urinate.

"Ah, right! Yes, I understand now! Swamp filth, you say? OK, that's fine, I can live with that. Can I go now, please?" Trying not to cry, Embram Ferret Frightener stood his ground and quietly asked his bladder to do the same. You see, if there was one thing he was more terrified of than fire, it was spiders. Small, hairy or very, very big like this one, it really didn't matter.

"If I had my way, lizard, you would now be part of my mid-morning brunch; but the council, in all its wisdom, seems to think otherwise! So, for now at least, you can safely assume that you are going to come out of this encounter unscathed and uneaten ... This time!"

If it wasn't for the fact that he was now jacketless, Embram would have been quite sure that it had all been just a bad dream. He was back outside, looking up at the *Angel Falls* complex, the taxi dimension-shifting behind him as it pulled away in search of another fare. Bathed in the soft, yellow glow of the street lamps, he shook his head in confusion and started to look for another cab, his limited imagination running riot as he tried in vain to understand what had happened. It was then that he noticed the small, white envelope he was holding, and the words printed on it in gold leaf lettering:

VERY PRIVATE AND CONFIDENTIAL

FOR THE PERSONAL ATTENTION OF
MR. EMBRAM FERRET FRIGHTENER, ESQ.

Opening the letter, he read the contents, re-read them, and read them again. Feeling what colour he had draining away, Embram Ferret Frightener placed the paper into his mouth, swallowed it, and decided he wanted his mummy.

Today had started out bad: but now, bad was just a word.

CHAPTER SEVEN

"Thank you for your prompt attendance, Gabriel. If you could please take a seat we can begin this very extraordinary meeting."

Fighting back the urge to ask where he was supposed to take it to, Archangel Gabriel nodded to the middle-aged woman sitting at the centre of the long oak table, and quickly glanced at the other six figures seated either side of her. Not recognising any of them, he folded his wings and sat in one of the two identical chairs arranged in front of the assembly. Against a background of whispered conversation and shuffling paper, he adjusted the angle of the sword and looked around the Chapter House. He had been just about everywhere in Heaven during his ageless life; in fact he was one of the very few divine beings ever to have been invited for breakfast by the *One;* but here, sitting in the Chapter House in Committee Block 3, he was as much a stranger as anyone else would have been. He was admiring the mock gothic splendour of the vast room when she spoke to him again.

"My name is Hewitt, Julia Hewitt, and I am President of the Celestial High Council, or committee, depending on which terminology you would prefer. I'm sure you are wondering just what this is all about? Well, before we get down to the reason you are here, let me introduce you to the members of this, the newly formed Joint Darkness & Light Emergency Committee, of which this is the first meeting. We will start at my far right with

Mr. Simon Sharp, who is Minister of Internal Affairs with our opposition colleagues on the Dark Council."

Gabriel automatically reached for his sword, drawing it quickly as he stood and advanced towards the fat, balding man.

"*The Dark Council?* Be thee gone foul creature from the black pit! Be thee gone before I send thee back from whence thee came!" (He hated the way he had to recite the same old antediluvian lines; it was such a cliché, but the demands for tradition were still strong amongst a certain element of Heaven's elite.) He was about to raise the sword when a shrill female voice stopped him.

"Archangel Gabriel! Will you please sit down, NOW! Mr. Sharp is here at the direct invitation of the Celestial High Council, and as such is under our personal protection! Is that quite clear?"

Looking directly at the woman, and then at the two obviously terrified Imperial Angelic Guards who had stepped between him and the Dark Council member, Gabriel sheathed the sword and sat back down.

"My apologies, Archangel, I should have explained things a little better when you first arrived. Forgive me if I ask for a little more patience on your part."

Settling back into the chair, Gabriel ignored the condescending tone of her voice, and refused to let the look of distaste leave his face as he stared at Sharp.

"As I was saying, if I may continue. Next to Mr. Sharp we have Councillor Rebecca Small, who is here representing our associates in the *Autonomous State of Purgatory.*"

Glancing at the small, young woman seated next to Sharp, Gabriel forced a smile and nodded slightly. Purgatory may not have been officially within the jurisdiction of the celestial host, but neither was it part of Sharp's territory.

"I am very pleased to meet you at last, Archangel.

Your name and reputation are somewhat of a legend in the independent states."

"More like 'infamous reputation'!" The new voice came from the bag attached to Gabriel's belt.

"I'm sorry?" The young woman looked at him. "What did you say?"

Reaching down and squeezing the bag, Gabriel ignored the muffled groan from its interior and shook his head quickly.

"It was nothing important, nothing important at all. And thank you Miss Small. It is Miss, isn't it?"

The young representative from Purgatory blushed slightly as she brushed her long brown hair away from her face, a gesture that revealed all five of her bright blue eyes.

"Yes Archangel, actually it is."

"Excuse me! We do have some extremely pressing business to attend to, so if you could all please pay attention!"

Once again the older woman had interrupted him, her pompous and condescending attitude beginning to make its mark on his already deteriorating patience. Gripping the hilt of his sword, and picturing yet another night light on his bedside table (he was also sure that Marcus wouldn't say no to a little company inside the bag), Gabriel seethed silently as Julia Hewitt's voice once again filled the room.

The introduction of the remaining four seated figures went without any further interruption, all of them turning out to be minor officials of the Celestial Council, and all well below the Archangel's status, or interest. When the preamble finally ended, Julia Hewitt and the other six committee members put on their best concerned faces, clasped their hands together in unison, and looked directly at him.

"Well, Archangel." It was becoming obvious that Julia loved the sound of her own voice more than anything else. "We now arrive at the reason you have been summoned to attend this extraordinary, and, I must add, very confidential meeting."

Realising just how much this woman was enjoying her brief moment of prominence, Gabriel finally decided that enough was enough.

"He's missing, isn't he?"

"Missing?" Unclasping her hands and sitting back in the chair, President Hewitt stared at him, surprise tinged with annoyance showing on her face. "What is it you know, Gabriel? And more importantly, how do you know?"

"Madam President!" He was going to enjoy this part. "Just *who* do you think you are talking to?"

"I'm sorry, I don't quite understand. What precisely are you saying?" Leaning forward and clasping her hands back together again, Julia Hewitt tried in vain to remain in charge of the situation and regain the upper hand, something she failed to do on both counts.

"Your council may have a modicum of power within the infrastructure of Heaven. It may even have a degree of power within the divine hierarchy. But, my dear lady, you know *nothing* about the true way of things! You are an insignificant cog in an infinite celestial machine."

"I beg your pardon! Just who do you think you are Gabriel?"

"*I*, Madam President? I am *Abruel—Jibril—Jiburili—Serafili*—take your pick! I am the one who sits at *His* side, and I am the keeper of Eden! (Whatever happened to those two? Nice couple … nice orchard!) I, *Miss* Hewitt, and I'm sure you *are* a Miss, I am your Nemesis! Your walking, talking, Armageddon! I, my dear Miss Julia Hewitt, *I* am your very worst nightmare and most painful memory rolled into one!"

Gripping the sword even tighter as he began to move from the chair, Gabriel spat out the words as rage filled him.

"But most importantly, Madam 'high and mighty council member,' it's me *He* listens to! Do you hear what I'm saying? *ME! ME! ME!*"

It was at this point in the proceedings that Julia Hewitt (actually Ms. Hewitt to be precise) gained back not only the upper hand, but the whole arm, torso and nether regions as well.

"That was quite a speech, my dear Archangel, quite a speech indeed. But there is one specific point which I feel I must clarify to some extent." President Hewitt sat upright, her self-confidence handed back to her by the Archangel's own words. "As you have so eloquently put it, Gabriel, you sit at *His* side, and *He* listens to you." She smiled openly, leaning back in the chair as she continued. "But as you have also stated, *He* is in fact missing!"

It isn't very often that someone of an Archangel's standing finds himself (or herself, to be politically correct) stranded up the proverbial creek without a dry set of wings. (Unless, of course, you count the time Archangel Michael decided to rename himself 'The Avenger', and dress in a one piece red spandex suit, complete with nylon cape, mask, and latex surgical gloves.) But this *was* one of those very rare occasions.

"You see, Gabriel, you and the rest of your heavenly host are all but redundant. There will be no place in the *New Democratic Republic of Heaven* for antiquities such as you and your kind, and when we eventually amalgamate with the Dark Council, a new era of prosperity and co-operation will dawn."

"Me! Redundant? Have you all lost touch with whatever celestial reality you live in? And what is all this rubbish about a Democratic Republic?" The Archangel's rage had dissolved as he listened to what was being said, his mind working overtime as his thought processes had difficulty in comprehending the treacherous nature of the situation. Determined to win back the upper hand, Gabriel resumed his verbal attack. "So if it's a revolution you and your council of traitors are planning to bring about, why do you need *Him?*" Looking back towards the end of the table, Gabriel glared at Simon Sharp. "And I am also willing to bet that the fallen one is missing as well, isn't he?"

"As a matter of fact the Dark Lord *is* temporarily indisposed, but that is of no concern to you, Gabriel." The corners of Sharp's grinning mouth joined at the back of his head. "He will be found and returned to take his rightful place, have no fear of that."

The grin returned to normal as he opened a folder that lay on the table in front of him. "And that, with the committee's permission, is where we explain just where you and your travelling companion enter the equation."

For an instant Gabriel glanced down at the bag at his waist. Travelling companion? How did they know about the head? But more importantly, what did they know and how long had they known?'

"Exactly what travelling companion are you talking about?" he said, deciding that simple ignorance was a far better plan of defence than admitting to anything unless he had to.

"As this is a joint venture, it has been decided to combine our resources and send two of our finest, to retrieve ..." Simon Sharp paused for a few moments, his grin growing once again as he searched for the right words, "...retrieve the goods, or the bads, depending on which side of the fence you are sitting on I suppose."

It has to be said that the number of times an Archangel (or any angel, when it comes to it) has known total confusion can be counted on no hands. It's just not an experience that comes easily to such beings; neither is it a state of mind generally understood in the usually well ordered kingdom of the hereafter.

Well that *was* the situation ... until now.

"This had better be some kind of cosmic joke!" Gabriel said, staring at the seven seated figures in genuine disbelief. "But just to clarify things, let me see if I have this right, Hewitt! You and your committee intend not only to take over the whole celestial establishment, but also to form a merger with *them*?" Pointing at Sharp, Gabriel's eyes narrowed. "Have you any idea what you are proposing? *They* are the dark ones. The foul spawn of evil, and servants of the beast! We have been at war with them since time immemorial, and that is the way it must always be! There cannot be any change in the status quo! No change at all!"

"My dear Gabriel, you really have no idea, do you?" It was Julia Hewitt who spoke again. "A new order has risen simultaneously in Heaven and Hell; a radical change of perception, and one which has been on the cards for a very long time. This is the beginning of a new tomorrow, Archangel; a time to sweep away the dust of obsolescence and bring about long awaited transformations in a great many areas."

"What do you mean by a 'change of perception' and 'transformations'? What gives you the right to even think such thoughts, let alone try and carry them out? It's always been *Him*. *He* is the word, the thought, the deed!" Anger flared. "And do you think the Heavenly army will just sit in its barracks while you undermine everything we have ever known and fought for? Do you really think that this revolution of yours will be an easy and a bloodless one?" (Actually not a very good choice of words, seeing as no creature in either camp could, in reality, bleed.)

Julia Hewitt examined a well manicured fingernail, shook her head and sighed.

"Tell me, Archangel, just how much power do you *think* you actually have in Heaven these days? Or how many times recently you have been called upon to unsheathe that sword of yours in *His,* or in fact, anyone else's name? The answer to both questions, Gabriel, is none, isn't it? I am correct, am I not?"

The Archangel's confusion started to sprout roots as she pushed home a point he didn't want to hear.

"And do you actually think that we haven't covered all avenues and possibilities? How many new promotions have you sanctioned over the past two millennia? How many young cadet-angels have you given early commissions, all on the recommendation of their commanding officers? The same officers who believe, like us, that change is long overdue."

Gabriel's confusion overwhelmed him, weaving its way deeper and deeper into his senses as he attempted to wake up from this sleepless nightmare (even though he had no real idea what a nightmare actually was, seeing as he had no need for sleep, so didn't dream in the first place).

"We have, thanks in no small part to you, Archangel, the army in our pocket. You see, as the commander of the Heavenly forces you have done an excellent job of instilling unquestioning obedience within the ranks; the unquestioning obedience of each soldier to the officers who command them. Those same officers who are now totally loyal to the council and the new values it promises to uphold."

As if reading the questions welling up in Gabriel's head, President Hewitt didn't give him the chance to interrupt her.

"And in answer to the first of the questions you are about to ask: as in all political ventures, compromise is often an unfortunate necessity. A republic is indeed our ultimate goal, but the need for a figurehead is a regrettable prerequisite for public stability in the early stages of any political change, is it not?"

"And my second question is?"

"Why do we need both of them back if amalgamation is part of the overall plan? It is, of course, a fact that like his counterpart, there is no real place for the Dark Lord within the structure of the new order; but our colleague, Mr. Sharp, also believes that it would be beneficial, for a limited period of time."

Not for the first time since his arrival, Gabriel gave serious thought to ending the insurrection by destroying the main protagonists while they were all assembled together in one place. It was as he slowly reached for his sword that he realised not just how many guards seemed to be in position around the room, but also how many were wearing sinister black Kevlar armour and fully enclosed helmets.

"I think, my dear Gabriel, that you should seriously reconsider your next course of action." It was Simon Sharp who spoke. "As you can see, we have pre-empted your more than obvious response. If nothing else, you and your kind are very predictable, and predictability is easily countered, is it not?"

It was clear that Sharp was enjoying this.

"I would, of course, personally introduce you to the members of our special forces who are kindly assisting us with security here today, but I'm sure there are still many questions to which you and your companion need answers."

"Yes! One of them being: just who is this bloody companion?"

Letting the grin join at the back again, Simon Sharp pointed to a spot behind the Archangel. "Allow me to introduce you to your partner in this undertaking. Archangel Gabriel, please say hello to Embardin Otter Culler."

CHAPTER EIGHT

He had simply just arrived, appearing in the large room a millisecond after reading the letter (mind you, in a place without time I suppose a millisecond could feel like a lifetime. But then again it's reasonable to expect that a lifetime in a place without time, could feel like a ... No! Maybe it would be better if we didn't go down that particular path). There had been no flashing lights or sirens, no 'Beam me up, Scotty,' and no pretty air stewardess bringing him duty-free drinks (or those little nibbles he so much enjoyed when he was watching re-runs of *The Sound of Music*). He had just appeared. Materialising in a room filled with heavily armed guards, standing behind two chairs, one of which was occupied by an angel.

"Ah, right! I'm OK! I think." The gargoyle was positive it was all down to jet lag (whatever that was), or the stilton cheese he had eaten last night for supper. Whatever it was that had caused these illusions, he was sure they would soon pass if he could just pass wind at either end.

"I'm where, you're who and what is he?" he heard himself start to babble as he pointed to the seated angel. "OK, it's him isn't it? Is it him? Or then again maybe it's not? Tell me it's not!" Embram started to dribble as realisation kicked him hard between the legs. "Could I call my mother please, and maybe my grandmother as well?"

Even in the wide awake coma he was now sure he

was experiencing, Embram registered the angel standing up, even understanding the act of a sword being drawn, but it was when the angel turned to face him that Embram Ferret Frightener finally let his bladder do its own thing.

"Oh! It is you! I've seen the posters, and I've watched you on TV. You seem taller. Can I have your autograph? It really is you, isn't it?" If gibbering had been a paid profession, he would now be reaching the position of managing director. Starting to quickly back away, the gargoyle winced as he collided with the pointed end of a guard's spear. "Nice wings! And I love the big sword! Does it take much polishing? I bet it's a pain having to carry it around with you all of the time. Can I hold it? The sword I mean!"

In his mind's eye he saw his head falling to the hard floor, bouncing around the room and ending up at the feet of the one he didn't want to be in the same dimension with, let alone the same room.

"Can I go now, please? Or would it be OK if I just removed my own head and gave it to you as a farewell gift? Yes? No? Why don't you just think about it, and in the meantime I'll just run away and bury myself?"

Now whether it was the sight of a 250 kilogram gargoyle hovering on the edge of insanity that stopped him using the sword, or the dozen or so black armoured guards who now surrounded them both that did it; either way, Gabriel had lowered the sword before a raised voice once again permeated the room.

"GABRIEL, you will sit down or I will ensure you are removed from this room forcibly! Do you understand?"

Julia Hewitt sat forward on the edge of her seat, her eyes wide and anger showing clearly on her reddening face.

"Both of you sit down this instant, do you hear me? I will not have this meeting disrupted any more. Is that clear?"

Her voice rose two more octaves as her anger took centre stage, her face now turning a worrying shade of purple as she glared at them both. She had partially composed herself by the time they had complied with her demands, her professionalism finally winning over her fraying emotions.

"Very well, now let us continue with the agenda in hand!" Opening a large manila file in front of her, Julia Hewitt withdrew two sheets of typed paper and handed them to the seated figures. "To start with, Gabriel, I would like you to formally meet your travelling companion for the extraordinary expedition you are about to embark upon." A smug, all-knowing smile had appeared on her face. "Archangel, please allow me to introduce you to ..." Gabriel stopped her in mid-sentence.

"Madam President, or whatever you call yourself! You continue to underestimate me, and that is not a wise thing to do, believe me. You see, none of you have any real idea how much I know, do you?" Gently patting the bag hanging from his belt, Gabriel silently thanked Marcus Enderholt the Third (oh well, here we go again ...) for keeping his mouth shut for the first time in two millennia. "Or if anyone else besides those of us formally present may have knowledge of this meeting."

The Archangel gave Julia Hewitt no chance to protest as he immediately turned to face the still terrified gargoyle.

"Correct me if I am wrong, but I believe you are Embram Ferret Frightener, gargoyle in charge of arrivals at the Rosewood Drive collection point."

A story is told amongst those who know (don't ask me who *those* are, because I really don't have a clue. All I know is that 'it's just told') that Archangels have an infinite knowledge of an infinite number of things, including a complete inventory of all that has been, and all that is to be. A built-in, divine encyclopaedia of infinite infinities: a broad database of information that can never become obsolete. It seems *they* were right.

Embram Ferret Frightener's bladder prepared to do its own thing yet again as Gabriel leaned across to him, whispering in his ear. "And don't worry, Mr. Ferret Frightener, your secret is safe with me. You see, I love dogs." The Archangel smiled again. "Even three headed ones!"

"Very well, let's play your little game, shall we?" Gabriel turned away from the now stunned gargoyle, and folded his arms. "*He,* or should I say *They,* are missing, and you want them found. Am I correct, Madam President?"

"Yes, that is the present situation, if you want to get down to basics." Julia Hewitt felt her self-confidence fading as she realised just how much she had underestimated the Archangel's shrewdness.

"And you want *Them* found in order to ensure stability while you carry out your plan to take overall control of both Heaven and Hell."

"Yes, we want the *One* found and brought back, but as I have said ..."

"Yes, Yes, I know! Mr. Sharp also requires the foul one found, but that part is of no concern to me!" Gabriel leaned forward. "But there is one thing I don't quite understand. Just how are you planning to deal with the others? Do you really believe that they will simply sit back and allow all of this to happen?"

"By others, I take it you are referring to the *Divine Host of Retired Deities?*"

Gabriel nodded.

"You still cannot grasp the overwhelming complexity of the situation, can you Gabriel? As with everything else, we have examined this aspect in great depth, and made contingency plans to neutralise their effectiveness in a number of very simple ways." Opening the manila folder again, President Hewitt withdrew a sheet of paper. "For over a millennium, both committees have gradually taken over most of the jobs others either didn't want to do, or found too mundane to bother with. You see, Gabriel, it's all to do with a universal truth ... no one wants to be responsible for the humdrum or tedious side of things, such as paperwork, or arranging appointments diaries for politicians ... or deities."

Continuing to read from the sheet, the woman's face broke into a grin.

"It seems that JC has an urgent meeting with the Pope. A meeting which his holiness will ensure includes an extended stop-over in the Vatican's best inquisition room." Gabriel listened in stunned amazement. "And it looks like Buddha is away on one of his soul-searching expeditions again: exploring for Nirvana, I believe." (It is rumoured that Buddha plays a mean grunge guitar ... or was it drums?)

"Impressed?" Julia Hewitt looked at the Archangel again, searching for any sign of insecurity. She saw none, so continued.

"Who's next? Ah yes, the Triple Goddess. Well it seems that the three of them are away enjoying a long overdue holiday. I believe they have booked two weeks in Benidorm with the *Pagan Package Tours Company*. Four-star hotel and free car hire—now that *is* value for money. As for the rest, well let's say they are all indisposed for the foreseeable future, and by the time they return it will all be over."

Gabriel managed to hide the unexpected feeling of admiration he found himself suddenly experiencing for this overbearing and conceited individual. No matter what his professional position, as a creature of power he couldn't fail to be impressed at the sheer audacity of the venture, or the scale of its apparent successes to date.

"So I take it that the general position in Hell is the same?"

It was Simon Sharp who answered his question, talking more to the silent gargoyle than to Gabriel. "Give or take one or two small problems that still have to be ironed out, our progress in the underworld is continuing at a similar pace. As you may have already gathered Ebinam, the internal infrastructure of Hades has begun to destabilise. Intake points have closed and members of the *Amalgamated Demons and Tormentors Union* have called for immediate industrial action."

For the first time since sitting down, Embram Ferret Frightener spoke. "The largest union in Hell is, coincidently, yours, I believe?"

Simon Sharp's grin spread. "I suppose it is my union in a manner of speaking, seeing as I do hold the position of Chief Shop Steward."

"Also the posts of Area Organiser, Membership Secretary, Vice President and President, if my memory serves me right!" Shifting position, the gargoyle folded his tattered wings tighter as he tried to find a more comfortable position within the restricted confines of the chair. "And for what it's worth, my name is Embram, Mr. Sharp! *E.M.B.R.A.M.* which spells Embram! It does not translate into Ebamin! Embarim! or even Elvis! So I would be grateful if you could please get it right, at least once."

Ignoring Ferret Frightener and his request, the representative from the Dark Council turned and spoke to President Hewitt. "I suggest, Madam President, that we dispense with the formalities and get down to the matter in hand."

Nodding, Julia Hewitt looked at the other committee members and then back to the two seated figures in front of her.

"I believe you are right, Mr. Sharp. This meeting has

gone on long enough and there is still much to do."
Looking directly at Gabriel and the gargoyle, the
woman paused for a moment, then continued. "It has
been decided by the councils that in the interest of
political correctness it would be prejudicial to
implement change within the structure of both houses
without the representation of, shall we say, the
managing directors. With this in mind, it has also been
decided that such an unorthodox problem calls for an
unorthodox strategy. There, gentlemen, is where you
enter the equation."

Embram felt suddenly uneasy: the headache imp
resumed its quest for oil in his head, while his
counterpart sitting next to him patted the bag on his
belt and just smiled.

"Through our differing contacts on the mortal side of
the great divide, we have narrowed the search down to a
medium sized city situated on a spheroid designated
within the E.A.R.T.H. classification spectrum."

Without thinking, Embram leaned over and whispered in the Archangel's ear.

"EARTH?"

"*Early Atmospheric Regeneration Through Hydro-
carbons,*" Gabriel whispered back, his eyes never
leaving Julia Hewitt. "One of *His* rare failures, and one
that's been a constant thorn in my side for what seems
like an eternity!"

Suddenly remembering just who he was talking to,
Embram pulled away quickly and pretended he had
never asked the question.

"With this information recently confirmed, a joint
decision has been made to dispatch you both to the
aforementioned place, where you will carry out the
tasks assigned to you."

"Is there any point in asking why us?" It was Gabriel
who asked the question that was on both of their
minds. "I can understand why you would want me out

of the way, as I'm sure the final phase of your plan will go much more smoothly without my presence to hinder you. But, tell me, why the gargoyle? It is a minor demon in a minor position, and it has no place on a mission such as the one you are proposing!"

"May I interject here, Madam President?" It was Sharp again. "You are correct, Gabriel, he is just a gargoyle, an insignificant minor demon with little or no worth whatsoever as far as I am personally concerned."

A cloud of steam escaped from Embram's flared nostrils; his lips curling back to expose sharp fangs as he clenched his fists tightly. He wanted to end it here and now, but the memory of Simon Sharp's real persona halted all thought of that.

"He was chosen simply because of his expendability, and if he fails in his part of the mission, which of course he will, he will be disposed of and no one will be any the wiser. Someone of your status, on the other hand, is a different matter; but as you say, things will go that much smoother here without your archaic views interrupting the proceedings."

The Archangel knew when he was cornered. "And, of course, you knew I couldn't refuse, didn't you? How can I? If I decline to find the *One* and persuade him to return, the coup will result in the complete annihilation of everything that has always been. Without *His* presence, and the support *He* is still able to call upon, everything we have ever known will be swept away in a tide of anarchy!"

"Now, now, Gabriel, is there any need for such an unfounded and alarmist attitude?" Julia Hewitt broke into the conversation. "The words 'coup' and 'anarchy' are *not* ones we on the council would choose to use. It will be a natural political progression from a dictatorship to a socialist republic. Do you really think that we would ever condone any form of ..."

Grabbing hold of the gargoyle's arm and pulling

him to his feet, Gabriel stood and stopped Hewitt in mid-sentence.

"Enough is enough! It's clear that neither of us has any choice but to do as you ask, so shall we cut to the chase and dispense with the rest of the crap? The gargoyle and I will find them both; and when we do, I will return and put an end to this traitorous insanity!"

"You will try Gabriel, that much we expect." It was Simon Sharp who replied. "But until your return, you *will* carry out your orders to the letter ... Do you *both* understand?"

Still holding the arm of the now terrified gargoyle (Embram was not sure whether it was the close proximity of the Archangel or the fact that the bag on Gabriel's belt was speaking that scared him the most), Gabriel turned and started to push his way through the massed ranks of guards surrounding them.

"Gabriel, wait will you? We need as much information as we can get to stop this!" It was the whispered voice of Marcus Enderholt that stopped the Archangel from fighting his way from the room. Looking at the expression on Embram's face, Gabriel knew he had also heard the voice. "Just have patience and listen to what else they have to say. It's just the three of us Gabriel, and we will need all the help we can get!"

"The four of us!" Embram Ferret Frightener looked from the bag to Gabriel, then back to the bag again. "There are four of us ... I think!" he said, wishing Fifi was there with him.

"I'll explain later," Gabriel said quietly. "I know it's asking the impossible, considering what we both are, but just trust me ... OK?"

Having little choice in the matter, his mind totally numb from the ongoing impossibility of the situation, Embram followed the angel's lead and turned back towards the two chairs. Sitting down, he tried in vain to wake up.

"Such outbursts are understandable in the circum- stances Gabriel, but please try to control yourself for a little longer if you could."

Pausing, Julia Hewitt nodded at a guard standing behind them before continuing.

"Before we close this extraordinary meeting, there is one other person I would like you to listen to. It is someone who, I believe, can give you a more pressing reason just why the task we have assigned to you is of the utmost importance to us all."

They heard the sound of a door opening and closing behind them, followed by footsteps approaching the long table. Before their curiosity could get the better of them, Embram and Gabriel watched as all seven seated figures stood up in unison.

"Gentlemen, I have the great honour and privilege to introduce you to Sir Adam the First, RIP., MIB., RSVP."

Embram bit through his forked tongue in a vain attempt to stifle the laugh, spitting out the severed pieces as he stared in disbelief at the new addition to the gathering now standing before them. Gabriel just stared.

"Don't you know it's rude to stare, Gabriel?" The effeminate but obviously male voice went well with the pink flared jeans, matching hair colouring and yellow Adidas trainers; as did the blue eye-liner and 1970's paisley-pattern shirt (just a minor point, but it's best to remember that in heaven gay still means happy).

"I'm sorry! Are we on first name terms?" The Archangel suddenly felt uneasy (which in itself was a first for someone who had no idea what uneasy was).

"Ah, of course, you don't recognise me out of uniform, do you? It's me, look! I'm the man with the big scythe, and no dress sense when it comes to hooded robes. Now do you know who it is?"

Scratching his re-grown tongue (it always itched when that happened), Embram Ferret Frightener's jaw dropped as realisation suddenly tapped him on the shoulder.

"You're kidding me! It is you, isn't it? It really is you!" Forgetting once again where he was and who was sitting next to him, Embram nudged Gabriel's arm and burst out laughing. "It's him, isn't it? It's the old bugger himself!"

"Come on Gabe, you're nearly there! Who am I? Come on, have a guess! If Mr. 'all teeth and talons' can get it right then I'm sure you can."

Sir Adam the first jumped about in front of the two seated figures, his obvious excitement drowning out any comments from the group still standing behind him. "Scythe, hooded robe and open-toed sandals? Come on! It's easy!"

"I don't believe it! Death! Is that you?" Like his companion, the Archangel failed to stifle the laugh. "Is this a joke? Why are you dressed like that, and what's with the hair?" Gabriel let his smile grow wider. "And what's with this 'Sir Adam the First' rubbish?"

"Unlike some, I do have a life outside work you know; and besides, have you ever had to wear sacking robes? No! I bet you haven't! Well, let me tell you, they make you itch from head to foot. I spend half my time scratching and the other half buying calamine lotion. And the Adam bit? Well, I was the first of *His* mortals, so who better to take on the job of Grim Reaper? In any case, seeing as there was no one else before me, who else could they have given the job to?"

"Ah, excuse me?" The voice was unfortunately all too familiar to Gabriel and Embram. "Could we please dispense with this inane chatter and resume the business in hand?"

Shrugging his shoulders, Adam the First blew Gabriel a kiss, smiled, and turned to face Hewitt and the others.

"Thank you, and can we please sit back down now?"

Nodding, Adam turned to face Gabriel and Embram,

thrust his hands into his pockets and sat down on the edge of the long table as the others re-took their seats.

"OK, I suppose I had better get down to the reason why I've been asked to come here. I know what's happening both here and down there, and I can't say I agree with it, but as an independent operative I have no say in how the political machine should, or should not, be run. So, as you can see, my hands are somewhat tied when it comes to taking sides; but what does concern me on a personal level is the increasing problem these disappearances are causing to my business and lifestyle."

"Problem, what sort of problem?" As a new voice joined the conversation, Gabriel grasped the bag hanging on his belt and squeezed. The new voice stopped abruptly.

"Who said that?" Julia Hewitt stood quickly and scanned the room for uninvited guests. "I asked who said that?"

"Ah, I'm sorry, it was me. I seem to have a frog in my throat, or it could be one of the toads I had for dinner. Would it be at all possible to ask for a drink of water?" Putting his hand to his mouth, Embram feigned a cough and winked at the Archangel. Gabriel smiled slightly, winked back, and gave the bag a harder squeeze. Only the two of them heard the muffled groan.

Taking the glass of water he was offered, Embram drank a mouthful and listened as Adam continued. "To cut what could be a very long story short, since the closure of both houses to new intakes, I find myself in a unique position, so to speak. In fact I find myself in a very difficult and extremely crowded position."

Pausing for a moment, Adam brushed back his hair, looked at his now pink hand and shrugged.

"You see, I now share my home with a multitude of misplaced souls, and believe me they are not the best of tenants by any stretch of the imagination."

Looking at his hand again and wondering if pink was perhaps a little over the top for a person of his standing, Adam shook his head and decided that it wasn't.

"I have souls living in my bathroom, my kitchen, all my bedrooms, my shed and my loft! I even have a race of extinct South American Indians squatting in my garage! I am inundated with the living dead, and more are arriving even as we speak. It's getting so bad that Eve would leave and go back to her mother's if she had a mother in the first place!"

Gabriel felt he had to ask. "Oh, you married her after all then? But does she know about the trousers and hair?"

"We have an open marriage, Gabriel, but that's none of your, or anyone else's, business! So are you going to take the mission or not?"

"Does she still make that amazing cider?" Gabriel looked at Embram, the gargoyle's sudden input to the conversation taking him by surprise.

"Cider? What's this about cider?"

"Eve's Eden Cider Company. Don't tell me you've never tried it? We used to have it imported; it sold in every bar in Hell until the Dark Council decided to tax it out of existence. All you can get now is *Jacks Ripping Rum,* made by the *Whitechapel Brewery,* a company which I believe is also owned by a certain council member."* Suddenly remembering the close proximity of Simon Sharp, Embram quickly added, "but the council know what's best for us, I'm sure."

Shaking his head in disbelief, Gabriel looked back to Adam First. "We have already decided to go, but let everyone here be clear on one very important point!" Standing up and pulling the gargoyle from his seat yet again, the Archangel walked the length of the table and looked at each seated figure in turn.

"We *will* find them both, and when we do we will

return and deal with this insurrection, and I will have all your heads brought to me on a silver platter!"

"He will you know, believe me, he will!" Everyone heard the voice from the bag, but this time no one took any notice.

"Well, Gabriel, that remains to be seen." Hewitt stared back at the Archangel. "But in the meantime, you will both be transported to the locale in question, so can we please ensure that your metamorphosis processes are complete before you arrive? I don't believe the living are quite ready to meet an Archangel again, let alone a minor demon from the Nine Rings of Hell."

Glancing at the gargoyle, Gabriel touched the hilt of his sword and spoke quietly. "All you have to do is remember who is in charge, demon!"

Looking past Adam First, Gabriel glared at the seven seated figures. "In the words of a very good friend of mine ... *I'll be back!*"

The last words they heard from Embram brought a smile to even Hewitt's lips: "Well, such is the afterlife ... Beam me up, Scotty."

PART TWO

'AWAY MISSION'

CHAPTER NINE

Gabriel slowly opened his eyes, winced and then shut them again, his head pounding as he waited for the spinning to stop. It always had this effect on him, even back when he was a regular visitor to this side of the divide. It was a brief but painful reminder that here in the physical realm any immortal being involuntarily adopted some form of corporeal trait. Supernatural transportation is an unsettling experience even for an Archangel.

As the spinning slowly receded, the headache settling into a hazy numbness, Archangel Gabriel opened his eyes and looked around. He was standing next to a statue of his friend Sir Edward Elgar (captain of the 'Angry Amazon' crib team, and Gabriel's paintball partner for the 1955-2002 season), itself located opposite an impressive example of Christian architecture. Cathedrals had always come very high on his personal list of favourite mortal achievements, mainly because they nearly always had a statue of him somewhere within their confines.

Looking up and down the dark street, he knew instinctively it was 4:00am on a winter's morning. Not by any divine revelation on his part, but by the fact that it was as cold as a vestal virgin, and that the little hand on a nearby clock pointed to the number four, while the big hand pointed to the twelve. Four in the morning and he was relaxed, confident, and alone.

Alone! He was alone! It hadn't registered until now,

but as the numbness faded, he realised he should have known better: knew he should have expected something to go wrong from the very beginning. Letting out a sigh of frustration, Gabriel looked up at the clear star-filled sky, and spoke aloud to whoever might be listening: "Why, oh why, did you have to choose a gargoyle?"

It was then that a voice reminded him that he did, in fact, have company of sorts. "Have we arrived yet? If we have, is there any slight chance that you could open this bloody bag?"

The voice emanated from the bag still hanging from his belt, a bag that Gabriel now reluctantly opened. Reaching inside, he grasped the head and pulled it out into the cold night; not at all surprised that the curls had already regenerated, but a little confused as to why they were now white.

"What's that? Is my mouth on fire?" The eyes of Marcus Enderholt the Third (Randy, Andy, Sandy, Mandy ...) widened as the head of the cherub was suddenly introduced to the freezing night air.

"That's called 'condensed breath'. It happens when you breathe out and your warm exhalation meets the cold air on a winter's night". Gabriel spoke quietly, knowing he was going to regret explaining the finer points of basic science.

"Breathing out on a cold night? Condensed breath? Have you got transportation sickness or something? You know I don't breathe, any more than you do!"

"It's your first time across the divide I take it?" Gabriel prepared himself for yet another round of explanations. "When you cross from our side to here, a part of you will always take on some form of mortal attribute. Take me, for example. I always get dizzy and suffer from the odd headache. Others discover they have bad teeth or halitosis, while a few, unfortunately, develop haemorrhoids."

"Develop haemorrhoids? What are haemorrhoids?"

"Never mind, it's better we don't go into that particular complaint too deeply. It's enough to say that your personal affliction is that you breathe."

For a moment the head pondered on the information it was being fed, the eyes watching the freezing breath as the mouth inhaled and exhaled faster and faster. It was as the eyes started to roll up into their sockets that the Archangel slapped the face.

"What? Who? Where am I?"

"And that, my friend, was called hyperventilating. It seems, Marcus, that breathing has one major disadvantage when it comes to acquiring it as an earthly characteristic."

"And that is?"

"If you stop breathing you stop existing."

The eyes widened.

"But I can't stop existing, seeing as I don't actually exist in the first place! So how can I stop? I'm a divine cherub, one of the celestial multitude!"

"Up there you are, I agree. But here, it seems, you are just a head."

"And why am I just a head? Why am I a mere fraction of my former self? Go on, answer me! Tell me Gabriel ... WHY?"

Considering for a moment the interesting possibility of the head becoming extinct by way of a hand clamped firmly around the now-breathing mouth, Gabriel let the thought find a niche in his mind, then lifted the head of the cherub to eye level.

"If, during the period of our stay on this side of the divide, you in any way piss me off, I swear that I will ensure that your present mortality will be the death of you! On the other side I only answer to the *One*, but here I answer to no one! Is that within your limited range of understanding?"

The head looked at the Archangel, its eyes narrowing

as it ran through the restricted number of responses it could safely use, considering the situation it found itself in. Finally, it chose the most logical one.

"Yes, I understand."

Gabriel was about to place the head back into the bag when a sudden thundering crash reverberated around the dark, empty street. The noise reminded him of the time Zeus had insisted that the Olympus Eleven darts team use his lightening bolts in place of their tried and tested arrows. Spinning round, and ignoring the screams of protest from the head as it made contact with the concrete plinth of the statue, Gabriel looked on in amazement as a large, green wheelie bin careered down the street towards him. Stepping backwards into the deserted road, he watched the plastic container hit the statue, tip on to its side and spill its contents in an arc over the immediate area.

"And just where have you been?" Gabriel said, speaking to the large pile of rubbish that was slowly crawling away from the disaster area. "You're late!"

As the mound of garbage slowly started to rise, the Archangel sighed and stepped forward, brushing away bits of dirt which had been blown in his direction.

"I had to get something first." Shaking off the excess litter, a human-shaped figure turned to face Gabriel.

"Your lot are a bunch of bloody amateurs! And they have the nerve to call themselves a transportation crew! They couldn't transport a sentence from their brain to their mouth!"

Closing his eyes and wishing he was back in a particular office drinking coffee, Gabriel dropped the protesting head back into the bag and rubbed his temples as the headache returned.

"Let me guess: it has blue fur, a cold wet nose, and it shits on the carpet!"

"Sorry, what has?"

"The thing you nearly forgot! You've brought the bloody dog, haven't you? That's what you meant by the 'four of us' back there at the meeting!"

As the late-arriving figure stepped into the light of a street lamp, a groan of despair escaped the Archangel's lips; a sigh that must have been heard across the length and breadth of both realms.

"Robbie Williams?" Gabriel shook his head and stared at the image of every teenage schoolgirl's fantasies. "You chose Robbie Williams?"

"Yes I did. Why, is there a problem with that? Robbie is as much a social icon as the person you have chosen to emulate in your own human disguise!"

"There is a universe of difference between a former boy band member and Sir Cliff Richard. In any case, you just can't walk about looking like him, and that's final!"

"Why can't I?"

"Because you just can't, that's all! Just change into someone else, and make it a less conspicuous transformation will you?"

"If you will, I will!"

"Who is the all-powerful avenging Archangel here, you or me?"

"You are."

"And who could remove your backbone through your mouth if he wanted to?"

"You could."

"Correct! So change now!"

A noise from inside the upturned wheelie bin stopped the argument. Now here is an interesting little snippet of trivia which may, or may not, be of use during those long cold winter nights playing the board game of a similar name:

Question: What is the one thing Archangels and Demons have in common?

Give in?

Answer: An irrational and overpowering fear of cockroaches.

A small but significant fact that goes a long way to explaining the signs of rising panic that suddenly showed on both of their faces as the noise increased.

"What was that?" Embram spun around, backing away from the green plastic bin. "What's making that noise?"

"Probably mice," answered Gabriel, backing away beside the one-time Take That singer. (Gabriel still thought that Gary Barlow had far more talent and could never understand what anyone saw in Robbie Williams; except, that was, for the tattoos! He had always fancied one saying 'DAD' surrounded by laurel leaves on his own arm.)

"Go and have a look and see what it is, Embram!"

"No way am I going to look! You're the Archangel, you look!"

Stopping at what they hoped was a safe distance, the Robbie Williams and Sir Cliff Richard look-alikes watched as a large mound of rubbish left the confines of the upturned bin and headed their way.

"It's one of them, isn't it?" blurted Robbie, grabbing Cliff's arm. "It's a cock-bloody-roach!"

"That's a bit big for a cockroach!" Sir Cliff said, trying to convince himself, if no one else.

"Then it's a lot of them! Maybe it's a cock-bloody-roach convention!"

Taking another two steps back, Gabriel tried very hard to maintain his calm and dignified persona. It only partially worked.

"You're right, I am the Archangel, and because of that unarguable fact, I am the senior one here … so you look!"

Before Embram 'Robbie Williams' Ferret Frightener knew what was happening, Archangel 'Summer Holiday'

Gabriel grabbed his arm, spun him round and pushed him bodily towards the moving pile of garbage.

As he collided with the bin Embram's memory, still fragmented from transportation, suddenly came back with a vengeance.

"Oh no, it's Fifi! How could I have forgotten?"

Falling to his knees and ignoring the tearing sound as his very expensive, but tight, jeans split from front to back, Embram started to dig away at the pile of moving rubbish, his pathetic whimpering bringing a feeling of despair to Gabriel as he watched the display of panic.

"Of course, it's the dog isn't it? Why am I not surprised, Embram?" The angel shook his head as he watched the gargoyle-in-human-form making a fool of himself.

Pulling away the paper, dirt and cigarette ends that covered the emerging canine, Embram scooped up the dog and walked back to where the Archangel stood.

"How could I have forgotten you?" Embram was babbling again as he cleaned off the last of the dirt. "This is unforgivable of me!"

"Enough is enough! Put the bloody animal down and stop whining, will you? We have a job to do, and the sooner we do it the sooner we can put an end to the council's disloyalty!"

Gently placing the blue-rinse poodle on the ground, Embram looked at his colleague and immediately noticed the difference.

"Where's he gone?"

"Where has who gone?"

"Mr. 'all teeth and smiles,' where is he?"

Resisting the urge to place a well aimed foot firmly into the opposite end of the dog that was now sniffing at his leg, Gabriel looked at Embram and suddenly felt very tired (another new experience, and one he assumed went with the headaches).

"I've changed my persona, and I would be grateful if you did the same. There is a great deal for us to do, and hordes of teenage girls chasing what they will perceive as the real Robbie Williams will only slow down our progress."

Looking at the Archangel's new disguise, Embram Ferret Frightener shrugged his shoulders and waved a hand in front of his Robbie Williams face. The transformation was instantaneous.

"We will wait in there until this side of the divide wakes up."

Pointing across to the towering edifice of the cathedral, Gabriel waited for the expected panic response.

"You are kidding me, of course! I can't go in there! Look along the walls, will you? Look at those stone faces and tell me what they look like to you."

"They look like gargoyles to me and, believe it or not, that's just what they are."

"Exactly, and you expect me to ..."

The world according to Embram Ferret Frightener's human eyes rotated 180 degrees and stopped; the new view, that of a pair of white Nike trainers, bringing a momentary sense of amusement to an otherwise confused mind.

He was hanging upside down, suspended from the outstretched hand of the newly transformed Gabriel, who now resembled a smiling ex-Police singer named Sting. The poodle, unsure of her master's new choice of position, promptly began to chew at the end of his nose.

"If it's all right with you, I would rather you turned me the right way up. I seem to be feeling a little odd like this, and you're confusing Fifi."

Ignoring the request, Gabriel turned and started walking towards the tree-lined cathedral grounds, Embram's continuing protests echoing round the deserted streets. They were suddenly replaced by an unrelated question.

"By the way, where's the sword?"

Looking at the upside-down face of his partner in crime, Gabriel frowned. "If you must know, I'm not allowed to bring it to this side of the divide any more!"

"Why? I thought you and it were joined at the hilt, so to speak."

"We were, but against my better judgement I let someone borrow it once and he threw it into a bloody lake when he was finished with it!"

"Someone threw your sword into a lake? Wait a minute, you didn't loan it to that King Arthur bloke, did you? I read all about him in the third edition of *Merlin's Definitive D.I.Y. Black Magic & Sorcery Manual.* So that was you in the lake? I didn't know angels could swim, let alone do it in a flowing silk medieval dress."

As the dawn chorus began to filter through the darkness, it was joined for a brief moment by the sound of a large wooden door closing. And the distant scream of a gargoyle with his head trapped momentarily on the outside.

CHAPTER TEN

It was 7:30am when they reached the shop; two middle-aged men bearing a striking resemblance to a famous pair of celebrities. The older one, dressed in an original series *Star Trek* uniform with captain's markings, searched in a small bag, impatience showing on his familiar face.

"Did I give you the keys this morning?" The question went unanswered for a moment, the other man scratching at a pointed ear and shaking his head in disbelief.

"No, you put them in your pocket, remember?"

The second figure, seemingly a Vulcan dressed in the uniform of the film era, with the rank of commander clearly visible, pointed to his friend's trouser pocket.

"You always put them in your pocket, so why do you continually refuse to look there first?"

Reaching into the pocket of his black trousers and apparently ignoring the obvious frustration in his friend's comment, Gerald Oliver Davies (Captain Kirk look-alike circa 1966) pulled out a bunch of well-worn keys.

"Did you lock the shuttle?"

Samuel Allen Trevor Anthony Nevis (Spock, circa *Star Trek VI: The Undiscovered Country*) ran a hand through his black hair and sighed. He heard the same question every morning, and gave the same answer every time.

"Yes Captain, it's locked down and docked in hanger bay three."

The shuttle was in fact a 1984 Ford Sierra, and the hanger bay a small car park behind a row of shops, situated in the northern part of the city (for the uninitiated, the area in question is a medium-sized city called Worcester, about 25 miles south of the sprawling metropolis of Birmingham, England). One of these shops, a small yet deceptively spacious building constructed during the reign of Victoria (Queen Victoria, not the pub depicted in a famous TV soap) being the pair's ultimate destination. A new venture, and only one amongst countless others on the street.

The name of this 'enterprising' business? *The Captains Log* of course! (Actually, it's a small cult TV shop situated in a slightly run-down area of this West Midlands city, and the roof leaks. But it's a living.)

Opening the door the two middle-aged men entered the shop, both trying to ignore the already substantial queue slowly forming outside.

"How long do you think they've been there?" the captain asked, as he switched on the lights, walked over to the alarm panel, and keyed in the six digit code.

"All night I expect. I've come to the conclusion that these Trekkers, Trekkies, or whatever they call themselves, don't sleep. They just exist in a world located somewhere between sanity and madness." Spock walked back to the door and looked out at the growing line of customers.

"It's a little pathetic really when you think about it." The captain spoke again, his mind now concentrating more on making the day's first cup of coffee than the conversation. "The way their whole existence is wrapped up in just one thing, I mean."

"It may be pathetic, Gerald, but it's also profit, and isn't that what business is all about? In any case, you have no room to criticise: talk about the saucepan calling the coffee pot a colour different to white!"

"It's 'the pot calling the kettle black'." Gerald Oliver Davies said as he walked over to the percolator. Filling it with a good helping of Bolivian coffee and switching it on, he smiled to himself as the expected comment came from the other man.

"What is?"

"The saying you are trying to use. It's 'the pot calling the kettle black'."

"Whatever! All I know is that you're the one who insisted our business venture should boldly go where no business has gone before, so to speak!"

Breathing in the rich aroma of the South American beans, the captain looked into the mirror hanging above the small coffee station and adjusted his face.

"And that's another thing!" The Spock look-alike took a last glance at the crowd and walked over to join his captain. "Do we have to look like this?"

Obviously happy with the result of his adjustments, Gerald looked away from the reflection of a younger James Tiberius Kirk and poured the coffee.

"Come on, Lucifer; it was relatively easy for you, wasn't it? You were half way there already with the pointed ears, upturned eye brows and black hair. Look what I have to do each morning. Face re-moulding plays havoc with my skin, and do you think I like gelling my hair?"

Handing the fallen (Spock look-alike) angel one of the steaming mugs, he walked across to the counter and looked around the interior of the shop.

Row after row of glass and chrome shelving lined the walls, filled with the paraphernalia of cult TV and film memorabilia. Books, magazines and plastic model kits, all illuminated by overhead spotlights, or positioned on their own impressive presentation stands. In one corner, opposite a full size model of the *ALIEN* (which always reminded Lucifer of a blind date he once had) stood a tailor's dummy dressed in the original uniform worn by Deforest Kelly in *Star Trek: The Motion Picture.* In another part of the showroom a Dalek guarded the counter, its rubber sink plunger holding a rare re-mastered compact disk entitled *Outer Space/Inner Mind.* (For those without any detailed knowledge of the finer points of *Star Trek* history, this was an album released by Leonard Nimoy in 1974, and one probably best forgotten.)

"Not a bad set up for two divine beings from the other side of the divide, is it?" Captain Kirk finished his coffee and smiled with satisfaction. "I think we have it made finally, don't you? No more worries about the so-called Heaven-Hell conflict, no more trying to please all the unions all of the time, and no more heavenly choir with their electronic harps, folk music, and falsetto voices."

"I suppose you're right, and I must admit that personally I don't miss the new craze for 1980's music that's sweeping Hell at the moment; but I will never, ever, get used to the cold. Any chance we can turn the heating up?"

Without waiting for an answer, the fallen one moved an index finger and smiled as the radiator behind him warmed parts of him only his mother had ever seen (although I use the term 'mother' very loosely: the law of averages dictating that someone must have loved him at some time). Looking at the *Star Trek* watch strapped to his wrist, that read '8:30am Earth Time', the Vulcan started to walk towards the door and the waiting customers. He was stopped by a hand on his arm.

"Are you telling me that you don't like Duran Duran?"

Looking at Gerald he frowned and asked a seemingly obvious question: "Why are you stuttering?"

CHAPTER ELEVEN

"Exactly where is the creature now?" The head of Marcus Enderholt the Third (just how a non-sexual cherub can be known as Randy is an interesting question, but one that's best investigated another time) asked the question as it was brought out of the bag and placed on the stone floor of the cathedral cloister. The Archangel was seated directly opposite on a wooden pew, once again resplendent in full armour. "And is it really wise for you to look like that in here? After all, Gabe, what if someone happens to see you?"

Allowing his wings to open as much as they could within the confines of the pew, Gabriel leaned forward and picked up the head, lifting it to eye-level as he slowly stood up, his eyes narrowing.

"Firstly, the name is Gabriel, and not Gabe! Do you remember me telling you that once before? Or should I spell it out for you again? G.A.B.R.I.E.L. It's a word which, when translated, means: 'I am a somebody,' and not a third-rate dogsbody like you! Secondly, do you see anyone else in here with us? No, of course you don't! On this side of the divide this is called 'early morning' and places like this are as empty as a suggestion box in Hell! Thirdly, the creature, as you so aptly call him, is cleaning up the shit left behind by his bloody dog. A pathetic animal, which it turns out isn't cathedral trained!"

"Yes she is! It's just that she's nervous, that's all." Out of the shadows stepped a teenage boy dressed in baggy, cropped jeans, dirty Adidas trainers, and a hooded sweatshirt emblazoned with a motif depicting a terrified looking ferret and the words 'Skateboarders Just Do It'.

Sitting down on the pew recently vacated by Gabriel, the skater boy shook out his mop of dirty brown hair, popped a well-festered blackhead and picked aimlessly at his runny nose.

"A very interesting choice of disguise, gargoyle, but why are you wearing a tea cosy on your head, and what in all the saints is that contraption under your arm?" The Archangel had turned to face the new-look Embram as he walked over to the pew, a look of genuine admiration growing on his face as he turned the head of Marcus Enderholt so it could also see the transformation.

"Why am I not surprised? Absolutely no finesse at all, but what can you expect from a lesser-than-less demon? At least where we come from one knows how to transform into something with a little bit more class!" A look of distaste painted itself on Marcus Enderholt's face as he spoke. "I know I can rely on you, Gabriel, to uphold our divine standards ... can't I?"

Seemingly ignoring the head (which in fact he was), the Archangel repeated his previous question, pointing at the skateboard now lying on the floor.

"I asked what's with the hat, and what is that thing you were carrying?"

"Hey, dude, leave my beanie and board out of this boring conversation, man! Just give me a twelve foot vertical and I'll show you what the board's for!"

"A 'dude'? You called me a 'dude'?" Gabriel's voice echoed around the empty cloisters, reverberating off the stone walls and cracking a number of the priceless stained glass windows in the process. "You actually called me a 'dude'!" Dropping the head, which bounced along the stone floor and ended up in a particularly dirty corner of the long passage, the Archangel reached out, grasped the young human form of Embram by the hood, and lifted him into the air. Bringing him closer, Gabriel spoke in a whisper.

"What precisely is a 'dude'?" His face softened slightly as another question suddenly popped into his mind. "And where precisely is the dog?"

The sound of wheels running on a hard, stone floor brought his head around just in time to see the blue-rinse poodle appear out of the darkness riding a fluorescent green skateboard. She was wearing a hooded dog coat emblazoned with the words 'Tried It But Didn't Like It'. Gabriel sighed, looked skywards and dropped the boy. It was starting off as a bad day, but he knew it was going to get a lot worse before it got better. If it ever got better!

Rubbing at his aching temples, the angel imagined two paracetamol tablets and grimaced as he dry-swallowed the bitter-tasting pills.

"I don't suppose that there is any point in asking you to reconsider your choice of attire, is there?"

Not really expecting an answer, the Archangel watched with growing apathy as the skater gargoyle practised his new found skills up and down the length of the cloisters, closely followed by the skateboarding poodle.

Tilting his head to one side and ignoring the muffled cries emanating from a pile of dirt in a nearby corner, Gabriel shrugged his broad shoulders, moved a finger and spoke quietly to himself. "Ah well, if you can't beat them!"

As a sound akin to a loud belch echoed round the stone walls, skater boy stopped suddenly, looked at the Archangel and smiled broadly.

"Hey! Cool dude, real cool!"

CHAPTER TWELVE

"Hey man! They look almost real! What do you hold them on with? Are they plastic or latex? Can I buy a pair? How much are they?"

A spotty youth in a home-made *Next Generation* uniform and carrying a plastic 3rd season phaser pistol reached out and pulled on one of Lucifer Spock's pointed ears, rough, half-chewed fingernails scratching the smooth skin as he tried to remove it.

"Wow! Oh boy! They really do feel real! Can I have a pair, and will you ..."

Samuel Nevis (film era Spock) contemplated, for a brief moment, eating the annoying amoeba from the inside out, while still ensuring that he kept enough of an appetite for the other dozen or so creatures that filled the confines of the small shop. Moving his head to one side, he blinked his dark eyes once and smiled as a look of horror and embarrassment spread across the teenager's face. As the others standing around the youth moved away from the source of the sudden, unpleasant smell, Science Officer Spock grinned as the youth grasped the stained seat of his trousers, turned, and fled from the shop in tears.

"Come on, Samuel; was there really any need for that?" Gerald (Captain Kirk to you and I) handed a smiling customer her change and turned to face his partner. "What is the one word you keep drumming into me? 'Profit', isn't it? They create our profit, so why do you continue to humiliate them?"

"Come on, Gerald, let's be honest here shall we? They talk a load of shite, so why shouldn't I give them a pile of it back now and again? Anyway, you have no room to talk: everything here is marked 'genuine U.S. import', but you and I both know none of it is! You bring it into existence yourself in the second floor storeroom, and then we sell it to these fools!"

Gerald winked and everything stopped, as time ceased to exist within the confines of the shop; frozen Trekkies suddenly looking like bizarre mannequins at some *Paramount* closing down sale. Rubbing his face with both hands and wishing it was dinner time, James T. took a deep breath before speaking again.

"How long have we been friends, Lucifer? I'll tell you how long shall I? We've known each other since a time before I even invented time. We were the first, and no doubt we will eventually be the last. So what's with all the bad vibes lately: after all, it was your idea for us both to give up the pressure and stress of being deities."

Thinking of Columbian beans, Gerald handed his friend one of the two hot mugs of coffee that appeared on the counter in front of them. "In any case, it's not technically a lie, everything is imported from the U.S. ... Up Stairs!"

"Very good, Gerald, very good indeed. That answer is one that even I would be proud of! Talk about twisting the truth to fit the facts. That's about as far from the truth as you can get without actually lying."

Realising that Samuel was, in a sense, correct, Gerald drank his steaming mug of coffee and winked twice. The shop returned to life, ending the conversation there and then.

It was a minute before 12.30pm when the young man walked into the shop. The excessive amount of pure white hair that reached half way down the back of his immaculate red motorcycle leathers and the smile, which emphasised his unusually long canine teeth, made him stand out from the rest of the customers. Looking around the crowded room, the youth made a beeline for the counter.

"Are you him?"

Gerald looked up from his copy of *The Trekkers Guide to Star Wars* and stared at the new customer.

"Am I who?"

"Are you him?"

Realising that this was going to be a longer conversation than he actually wanted, Captain James T. shut the book and contemplated closing early.

"Shall we try again? Who is it you are looking for?"

"Are you him?" The young man's voice was starting to reflect the impatience he was now obviously beginning to feel. "I have to ask for him! They told me he would be here when I arrived!"

Thinking 'empty shop,' and wishing Lucifer hadn't chosen this particular time for his dinner break, Gerald was a little perplexed when the youth failed to disappear with the rest of the customers. (Although, to be honest, he wasn't that surprised considering the stress he had been under for the past millennium. Maybe it was just a case of omnipotent droop, he thought.)

"Are you him?"

Gerald took a deep breath and considered using good, old-fashioned violence to rid himself of this annoyance, his omnipotent mind settling as he contemplated the idea. Finally, deciding that such an act would, in theory at least, contravene a law he himself had laid down on certain stone tablets, he smiled his best smile and tried to speak as calmly as he could.

"Tell you what, let's try it another way, shall we?" Placing both hands on the counter, he looked at the youth and spoke again to the shop's only remaining customer. "Hello, and what can our friendly and helpful staff at *The Captains Log* do for you today?" Rediscovering the knowledge that sarcasm can be fun, the captain continued with the sales patter. "Could I point out our unbeatable selection of *Star Trek* DVDs? Or maybe interest you in a full set of *Next Generation* crew autographs? No? Very well then, could we possibly bring Sir's attention to our unique collection of plastic *Enterprise* model kits?"

"Are you he?"

"WHO IS HE? AND WHAT DO YOU WANT WITH HIM?"

The overwhelming urge to ignore what he had forced upon Moses returned as he wished he had added, 'unless someone really pisses you off,' to the rule about 'Thou shalt not kill.' As he finally decided that violence could well be an option after all, another voice joined the conversation.

"Ah, Mr. Rawith! I'm sorry I was out, but I do have some good news for you."

Walking over to the leather-clad youth, Samuel reached inside his film era uniform jacket and produced a large brown envelope.

"Here are the tickets I promised, and I hope you enjoy the convention."

Placing a hand on the arm of the youth and slipping the brown envelope into the top of his leathers, Mr. Nevis led him towards the open door and out into the street, pointing at the packet and nodding in answer to an obviously asked question.

" 'Bye, and have fun."

Re-entering the shop, Nevis brushed back his black hair and walked up to the counter where Gerald was standing with a puzzled look on his face.

"Convention tickets? What convention tickets?" James T. studied his friend with a look of surprise tinged with annoyance. "How come I didn't know about this? And how come we're not attending?"

"Don't panic, it's not until later in the year and I've already booked a table in the trade hall for us." Nevis leaned against the counter and smiled. "And I have also arranged for you to have dinner with the convention's special guest, George Takei."

Two large glasses of malt whisky suddenly appeared in his hands and a broad smile spread across his face.

"The only original crew member I haven't met! Wow! What can I say? A surprise dinner with George Takei, a trade table and even more profit for the business! Thanks Luce, and I really do mean thanks."

Watching the smile on his colleague's face grow, Lucifer Spock reached out a thin hand towards one of the drinks and listened as the captain continued. "If only the others knew the real truth behind you and I, and the way we originally started both domains together." Handing Satan one of the glasses, and drinking from the other himself, Captain Kirk continued his nostalgic trip down memory lane. "Can you imagine the chaos in both houses if they ever found out that you and I have always been friends, and that we were the ones who wrote the original history books?"

As the everlasting glass of malt started to take its toll (obviously Gerald's little affliction on this side of the divide was an inability to hold his drink), Lucifer nodded in the right places and wondered why the shop was empty.

"Do you ever smile?" The disjointed and unexpected question brought a genuine look of surprise to Lucifer's face.

"Smile? What do you mean 'do I ever smile'?"

"Do you ever smile when you hear all those Scandinavians and Greeks going on about their old religion? You know what I'm talking about; Olympus, Zeus, the Goddess, Thor and Odin. All those so-called 'old faiths'. If only they knew the real truth! If only they knew we were the first on the scene, so to speak, and we were the ones who created everyone, and everything, that came after us! Can you imagine their faces if they found out we run both provinces together?"

"You're drunk, so maybe we should end this conversation here and now. No one has any idea about any of that, and that's the way it must stay!" Blinking twice, Lucifer replaced the glasses with two mugs of steaming black coffee and looked around the quiet shop. "And where is everyone? It's gone 1.30 and look at the place: its empty!"

Feeling a little guilty, Captain James T. took the coffee, drank it down in one go and coughed lightly into his hand. Once again the shop was full.

CHAPTER THIRTEEN

It must be a sign of the times that no one takes any notice of a blue-rinse poodle in designer sunglasses riding a fluorescent green skateboard, weaving its way through the early morning shoppers. (The lack of response to its uncanny ability to bark in tune to Robbie Williams' *Millennium* does make you wonder, though!) So it's not really surprising that the two figures following the performing canine went almost unnoticed in the hustle and bustle of the busy street.

"Cool, dude, you look really cool!" First walking behind, then circling round his companion, the new-look Embram, skateboard balanced precariously on his head, walked backwards as he admired Gabriel's latest transformation. "A bit late 1970's retro, but cool all the same."

Dressed in an immaculate grey pinstripe suit, Union Jack *Doc Marten* boots and sporting an eight-inch red, white and blue Mohican hair cut, Archangel Gabriel shook his head and tried to ignore the rattle made by the multiple piercings that adorned his face.

"Well I'm glad you approve, but if I ever hear you use the words 'punk' or 'dude' in reference to me or how I look, I will ensure that the dog and you become permanently one with each other! Is that perfectly clear?"

Flipping the skateboard to the ground and stepping on to it, skater gargoyle started to follow skater dog through the steadily building crowd of people, his voice trailing away as he gained on his four-legged (or four-wheeled) pet.

"No worries, man! The word 'punk' will never pass my lips, and I swear that the fact that you look like a 'punk' rocker will never influence me into calling you a 'punk' ... Or a 'dude.' "

Gabriel watched in subdued amazement as Embram the skater skilfully negotiated a group of camera-laden Japanese tourists and continued on his way along the high street, weaving in and out of shop doorways and performing for a crowd that took little, if any, notice of just another spotty youth.

Shaking his head again, he immediately regretted one part of the transformation as it spoke directly into his left ear.

"Pathetic, isn't it?"

Attached to the punk angel's left earlobe by a gold chain, its white curls now gelled into spikes and its face enhanced by black mascara and dark purple lipstick, was the now somewhat shrunken head of the cherub Marcus Enderholt the Third. (Sorry, no more 'Randy to his friends' or anything else like that ... I refuse to continue along those lines! Well, at least for now, anyway.) The sing-song, Americanised voice was just as annoying as ever. "Just what does it think it's doing?"

"He tells me it's something called a 'kick flip'; and you have to admit, he's not bad, is he? Not bad at all."

"Not bad!" The voice in the punk angel's ear went up an octave as Gabriel picked his own way through the Japanese tourists. "What do you mean 'not bad'? He's obviously unaware of the immense importance of this mission. Or he just doesn't care! Either way, we would be better off without the disgusting creature and its foul smelling blue hell-hound!"

"That, Enderholt, is just an opinion, and not a very important one at that. Like it or not, the gargoyle is part of this mission, and that's the way it's going to stay! So either shut up or stop breathing. The choice is yours, so choose carefully!"

The head chose the former.

A growing crowd of spectators stood laughing and shaking their heads in amazement, their combined attention momentarily captured by the blue-rinse poodle barking in tune to a succession of Robbie Williams hits as a spotty youth performed tricks on a skateboard while collecting money in his beanie hat. Opening the top of his red leathers and brushing back his white hair, the teenage biker slowly pushed his way to the front of the crowd, his bright blue eyes scanning the area around and beyond the impromptu street show. Pulling out a large brown envelope and removing two sheets of paper, he glanced quickly at the first one, then continued his intense visual search. A search that didn't last long.

No one noticed when the clear blue eyes of the leather-clad youth changed to an impenetrable black. Neither did they hear the low guttural chanting as he stared directly at the approaching punk rocker with the red, white and blue hair. A sudden cold wind made those standing close to him in the crowd shiver. The approaching Archangel felt all of his immortal existence momentarily shift.

Gabriel felt as if his very spiritual essence had been, for a fleeting moment, torn away from him. Pulled out from deep within his very being; and for a split second of mortal time he felt a pain the likes of which even his divine imagination had never believed could exist.

Skateboarder Embram had just pocketed the collection of coins when he saw it happen. He had glanced up and seen the punk angel approaching as Fifi was finishing the final chorus of *Rock DJ*. What he saw seconds later brought a surge of native knowledge and instant recognition rushing to the forefront of his mind. With a sudden fear growing inside him, Embram picked up the poodle and skateboards and ran over to where a stunned and disorientated Gabriel was leaning against the wall of a building, his eyes tightly shut as he tried to steady himself against the brickwork.

"Are you OK?" Leading the dazed angel to a nearby bench, Embram helped him as he slowly sat down. "Put your head between your knees. I read somewhere that it helps your circulation at times like this."

"I don't have a circulation to help, idiot!" Pushing the spotty youth away, the punk Gabriel fought back the urge to vaporise the blue-rinse poodle that was now licking his face. "And will you get that creature away from me?"

Placing Fifi on the ground next to the skateboards, Embram walked away from the bench and looked around the busy street. His eyes darted this way and that, and a look of bewilderment crossed his face as he spoke quietly to himself. "It was one. I'm sure of it, but how could it have been? No, it's impossible! I would have known instantly. I would have been able to tell right away!"

Rubbing his temples in a vain attempt to ease the pounding headache that now seemed to fill his whole head, Gabriel looked at the skater gargoyle who appeared to be getting even more perplexed as he looked around the crowded street.

"What are you babbling about? What would you know?" Standing up, the Archangel waited for the ground to stop spinning, then slowly walked over to the puzzled-looking youth.

"What in *His* name just happened to me, Embram? What is it you know?"

"Well, I know what I think happened, but I also know I must be wrong!"

As the headache worsened, Gabriel lost all the patience he never had in the first place, grabbed the hood of Embram's top and lifted the spotty skateboarder towards him. With passers-by trying hard to ignore the obvious problem, Gabriel spoke directly into Embram's ear, his voice menacingly low.

"Do you remember Sodom and Gomorrah? Or how about those exquisite plagues of Egypt that became so popular? No? Well I'm sure you remember what happened to Atlantis, don't you? Well? Do you?"

Drawing the boy closer, Gabriel tightened his grip on the hood and snarled at the dog that was now sniffing around his feet. "And what about Bruce Willis and his *Die Hard* trilogy? Or that one of his about the mortal kid who could see the dead, but Bruce didn't know he was actually dead himself until the end of the film?"

With wide eyes, skater Embram looked at the punk angel and smiled. "Bruce Willis? What about Bruce Willis? Is he one of yours? Wow! I never would have guessed. Is he missing as well?"

For a brief moment Gabriel contemplated divine suicide. Falling on to his own sword had always appealed to the Japanese side of his nature (well, to be honest, the only Japanese part of this particular Archangel was a passing fad for Bonsai trees he once had after watching *The Last Samurai*). But seeing as he didn't have the *Sword of Retribution* with him the impulse was irrelevant and he pressed on with the seemingly pointless conversation.

"No of course he isn't, on both counts, you idiot! What a stupid question to ask! I just like his films, especially that one about the end of the world on this side of the divide. You know the one? That bloody big piece of rock slams into the mortal realm here and makes more of a mess than Noah remembers ... Oh, what was it called again?"

"*Armageddon*, I think," answered Embram, still unsure what this had to do with what had just happened.

"Yes, that's the one! I thought the special effects far surpassed the ones in *Deep Impact*, and ..."

The headache angel, who was now singing and dancing in his skull, decided that enough was enough and brought the matter in hand back into Gabriel's thoughts with a vengeance.

"Anyway that's not what we were talking about! Tell me what happened just then? You seem to know more than you are willing to say, gargoyle, and that is not a wise policy on your part! Just remember, it was me who was responsible for those acts of divine vengeance, and they're nothing compared to what I'm really capable of!"

Still not completely sure what the angel was talking about, Embram shrugged his shoulders and carried on. "Well I think I know what just happened, but then again I'm not totally sure. You see, nothing seems quite right, but then again it does, if you get my drift."

"Get your bloody drift? Unless you start talking sense I will ensure you are set adrift, in limbo, for an eternity. And then I'll make sure that bloody animal of yours is stuffed and mounted on my bedroom wall!"

Ignoring the indignant whine coming from Fifi, whose hooded dog coat now read 'I Would Like To Try It Again, But I Don't Have The Balls', Gabriel brought Embram's face even closer to his own.

"Now, sulphur breath, exactly what is it you know?"

Dropping Embram back on to his feet, Gabriel watched impatiently as the teenager adjusted his hood and popped a new spot.

"It was a wraith spell."

"What was a wraith spell?"

"The spell that almost turned you spiritually inside out ... but then again, it couldn't have been."

"Embram!"

"OK! OK! I know, limbo and all that. Well it was a wraith spell: I've seen enough of them to know that much for sure, but if it was then something is very wrong."

"Wrong? What do you mean by 'wrong'? Either it was a wraith or it wasn't, and if it was, what is it doing on this side of the divide?"

"All I know Gabe ... sorry, I mean Gabriel ... is that I didn't sense it. If it was a wraith, then I should have known the moment it arrived here in the mortal realm; but I can't sense anything unusual here at all. Except for the usual imps and minor demons that are just starting the early shift, there is nothing out of the ordinary here. As far as I'm concerned, everything feels normal."

For a brief moment Embram thought he saw a look of fear wander quickly across the Archangel's pierced face. Then it was gone.

"So, you tell me what happened just then. It felt as if I was being torn apart and scattered to the four corners of wherever it is parts can be scattered to!"

"Look, I really have no idea Gabriel! I'm just an arrival point gargoyle from a long forgotten region of the underworld. All I do know is that it was a wraith spell, cast by a wraith which isn't here."

Climbing onto his skateboard, Embram Ferret Frightener watched as Fifi Lamoure adjusted her designer sunglasses before jumping onto her own board. Picking his nose, Embram looked at the angel and shrugged his thin shoulders.

"In any case, as you are so fond of saying, you're the Archangel so you figure it out!"

Pushing off, both boarders started to make their way through the crowd and down the main pedestrian thoroughfare. As they disappeared from Gabriel's view, he heard Embram's voice above the noise of the street.

"Oh, and by the way, I think the head's dead."

CHAPTER FOURTEEN

He watched as his target started to fleetingly phase out of immortality, the very essence of the Archangel altering as the spell took effect. When it was over the caster would cease to be: the mission his only reason for existence, the spell a suicide weapon of divine mass-destruction. The task itself had just been completed when it happened. The wraith's eyes were changing from blackness back to bright blue when someone pushed him from behind.

"You're blocking my view, freak, so either move or your face will match the colour of those power-ranger leathers of yours!"

As his chanting ceased, the wraith replaced the en-velope in the top of his red leathers and slowly turned to face the reason for the interruption.

"Are you deaf, dipstick? I said move!"

The cause of the disturbance was two shaven-headed youths in combat trousers, black leather jackets and heavy work boots who now stood facing the white-haired biker wraith. Both sported 'Cut Here' tattoos around their ample necks. Tilting his head to one side, the biker wraith studied his adversaries in silence.

"So, are you a tough man in a set of fancy red leathers or just a dick without a dick? Either way, I think you have a need to give us your wallet!"

It's surprising just how quickly a crowd of people can disappear when trouble arrives, but it's less of a surprise just how many of those that are left who can suddenly become both blind and deaf at the same time.

Shaking his head and pushing past them, the biker wraith smiled a canine smile as he heard two sets of heavy footsteps follow him into the narrow confines of a deserted alleyway between two shops.

"Hey, Dickhead! Did we say we were finished with you? No, I don't think so, you little shit! You could have just given us your wallet and walked away, but no, you had to play the hard man! Well now you're going to wish you were never born!"

As a tattooed hand grabbed his shoulder, forcing him to turn round and face his attackers, the biker wraith's canine smile grew ... along with his teeth.

The last sound either of them heard before their instant journey into torment and oblivion (or at least its temporarily-closed arrival point) came from the mouth of their own private nemesis. "Unfortunately for you both, birth is a luxury I never had!"

As a liquid blackness engulfed them, the alleyway was empty once again.

At that precise moment a few streets away ...

"Remind me just *why* we are closing early today, Gerald." Samuel (Lucifer, Beelzebub, Lord of the Flies or Science Officer Spock, depending on your point of view) checked the locked door and followed his business partner to the car park at the rear of the building. "In fact, remind me why we close early every Wednesday."

"You know perfectly well, Samuel. If we close at the usual time, we miss the week's episode of *Voyager* on terrestrial TV, and a good half of *Deep Space Nine* on satellite."

Unlocking the driver's door, Gerald climbed in to the Sierra, reached over to the passenger door and let his friend into the car.

"OK, I understand the surreal reasoning behind it,

but please explain just why you need to watch it on TV when we have every episode of every *Star Trek* series on DVD!"

Starting the engine of the Ford and pulling out into the steady flow of afternoon traffic, Gerald (now in full dress uniform, circa original series, 1967) thought *'Pink Floyd—Dark Side of the Moon'* and relaxed in his seat as the car's CD player burst into life.

"Why do you think I had television invented in the first place? As an all seeing, all knowing deity about town, I foresaw the coming of *Star Trek.*" (But not unfortunately, it seems, *Blake's 7.)*

"I see. So working on that premise, I take it that you also foresaw the coming of the Black Death?"

"If I remember correctly, Lucifer, that particular little public relations exercise was one of yours. I seem to recall a very lucrative business venture you became involved in around that time, if my perfect memory serves me right, which it always does. 'Rent a shroud', I believe it was called."

No longer finding any enjoyment in what was turning into a difficult conversation, Lucifer Spock settled back in his seat, cast a minor irritation spell on a nearby group of nuns and made a virtual-reality phone call in his head.

CHAPTER FIFTEEN

"What's it feeling like now?" The spotty youth's voice echoed around the empty cathedral as he stroked the sleeping dog on his lap and oiled the wheels of the boards that hovered in front of him. "Still hurting?"

It had taken three hours of mortal time for Gabriel to feel steady enough to walk the relatively short distance back to the towering edifice. Three hours spent in contemplation, trying to accept the fact that he was suddenly very vulnerable and a very long way from home. And to add to the already mounting list of problems, the head wasn't dead, it was something far worse. It was missing.

"Yes! it hurts, and no! I'm not all right!" Rubbing his pierced face with both hands, Gabriel let his head fall back and gazed up to the ceiling of the cathedral. "Are you positive it was a wraith? If it was, how did it have the power to affect me? I'm an Archangel, for pity's sake, one of the ancient and powerful ones!"

Letting both skateboards descend slowly to the stone floor, Embram gently placed the sleeping poodle on to the seat next to him and turned to face the angel.

"I *know* it was a wraith spell, and seeing as only a wraith can cast a wraith spell, it must have been a wraith that cast it." Confusion had obviously paid a sudden visit to skater gargoyle's mind as he realised what he was saying. "I mean, if it wasn't a wraith, then how could something that isn't a wraith cast a wraith spell without a wraith's permission?"

"Embram?"

"Yes?"

"Shut up!"

Embram obliged.

It took most of the night and the early part of the morning for the disjointing effects of the spell to finally disappear. As Gabriel's mind struggled to focus on the sudden and disturbing introduction of an un-expected factor into the equation, the alarm on his Rolex watch realised it was 7am. (Actually the validity of the watch's Rolex pedigree had always been in question, in large part due to the fact that it had been a gift from a certain disgraced American ex-president.) Gabriel looked at the sleeping youth and dog and pondered on the other unforeseen problem that had arisen the previous day: the fact that the head wasn't dead (well, not as far as he knew at present), but was in fact missing.

To insult a cherub was, in certain quarters, expected from an angel of his divine rank and position in the heavenly host. To remove the same cherub's head using the *Sword of Retribution?* Well, that could poss-ibly be explained using a little thought, celestial guile, and a lot of heavenly luck. But to lose that same head? Now that was a different matter, a very different matter indeed! Somewhere on the other side of the great divide the plump and headless body of a cherub wandered, its immediate aim being to find the missing portion that gave it a mouth to complain through. And the one thing this particular cherub excelled at was complaining!

Touching the empty chain hanging from his ear, the punk Archangel Gabriel was about to rudely awaken the sleeping pair when the phone in his head rang.

"It's about time! Do you never answer your phone? All I've been getting, for the past who knows how long, is your voice mail!"

"Enderholt, is that you?" The Archangel made sure the relief he suddenly felt was not reflected in his voice; the worrying thought of having to explain the loss to the *One* thankfully disappearing from his mind. "Where in *His* name are you? How in Hell's supermarkets did you get there? And what are you actually doing?"

"Well that's just about the sort of reception I expected! Here I am, risking my immortality for you and your bloody mission, and all you can do is moan and groan, as usual! Can't you for once say something like, 'Hi Marcus my old mate, how's it hanging?' Or maybe, 'Randy, I've been out of my mind with worry, are you OK?' No! Of course you can't, you pompous, winged creep! All you can do is cut my frigging head off, stick it in a foul-smelling bag and force me to join you on yet another one of your 'fight the foul armies of darkness' crusades! Well, let me tell you something, you flying asshole! Let me tell you a few home truths ..."

"I'm sorry Marcus, my dear old friend." Gabriel's voice was calm as he interrupted the continuing barrage of insults that poured from the virtual phone in his head. "Can I ask you to do me one small favour?"

"Depends what it is, of course, but I suppose so!"

"Shut your mouth, before I remove your pathetic little existence from any form of reality it has ever known!"

The phone went quiet.

"Ah, that's better! Now, where was I? Ah yes, I was asking you where you were, how you got there, and what you were doing."

The sound of the now more subdued voice of Marcus Enderholt brought a smile of self-satisfaction to Gabriel's lips.

"At the moment I'm trying very hard not to vomit. I seem to be inside the pocket of a wraith in red leathers, and it's just as smelly in here as it is in your bloody bag!"

"A wraith? You know it's a wraith? How do you know? Even the gargoyle couldn't sense it on this side of the divide!"

"There you go again, underestimating anyone who isn't in your precious little army of light! I may not be an angel, but I do have contacts in certain quarters, if you get my meaning."

"No, I don't get your meaning. Just tell me what you know, or I will terminate this call *and* you at the same time!"

"It's a prototype Mk. 3A."

"What is?"

"The wraith!"

"OK, so what's a Mark Threehay?"

"No, Gabriel, it's pronounced *'Mark. Three. A'!*" Frustration was beginning to appear in the voice of the cherub. "The Mk. 3A wraith was a prototype. A new model designed specifically for stealth operations and internal security within the confines of Hell itself, but it was never used. That's why the lizard had no idea it was there. No denizen of the underworld can sense it."

"OK, so how come you know so much about all of this? Or is there something about *you* we need to know, Enderholt? Like where do your real loyalties lie, for example?"

Marcus Enderholt sighed before answering, his eyes rolling in their sockets as he tried to retain what little composure he had left.

"Now there's a surprise! How did I guess you would say something like that? No, Gabriel, I am not some kind of mole spying for them!" Even as he thought the words, Marcus couldn't stop the picture of a small, furry creature in a dinner suit, drinking a martini (shaken, not stirred), before driving off in an *Aston Martin* appearing in his mind. "Neither am I selling heavenly secrets to finance an expensive lifestyle! It just so happens that a certain fire imp I know ever so slightly works in the *Hades Research and Development Laboratory,* and this same imp has quite a fetish for clip-on angel wings. So, as no doubt you have already guessed, I sometimes help him to indulge in certain fantasies in return for information which may, or may not, be of use to me at some point."

Gabriel shook his head and smiled, not in disbelief, but once again with guarded admiration at the extent of this cherub's (and now partly his) business empire.

"Very well then, tell me what you know!"

Feeling one step ahead of the Archangel, Marcus Enderholt (or, to be precise, his head) informed Gabriel of the facts he had concerning their common foe. (Free of charge, of course. It was better, the cherub thought, not to push things too far!)

"Well, that's all I know on that particular subject, but there is one more small bit of information which *may* be of some use to you. It seems to be sleeping."

"Sleeping? Since when does such a creature need to sleep?"

Scanning his memory banks, Gabriel thought back to the beginning of everything, trying to recall anything concerning wraiths, their sleeping habits and whether they indeed needed to sleep in the first place. The search turned up nothing.

"It looks as if you are our eyes and ears in the enemy camp, Marcus, so see what else you can come up with. Contact me when you find anything; and find some way to get back, is that clear?"

"Eyes, ears, and a mouth: that's *all* I am thanks to you and your precious sword! You are going to have a lot to answer for when we get back, Gabriel, and don't think my union is going to allow any internal investigation and subsequent whitewash to take place! Do you understand me Archangel?"

"Marcus?"

"OK! OK! I know the bloody drill by now! It goes

something like, 'Shut up, you insignificant little anal worm and do as you're told!' Am I right? Yes, of course I'm right!"

The virtual phone in Gabriel's head went dead.

Waking the snoring Embram, Archangel Gabriel waited patiently while the spotty youth took the skater dog outside to pee, and then less patiently when the obnoxious adolescent decided that he also needed to go. Using a good, old-fashioned threat of physical violence to remind him that gargoyles have no need to pee no matter what disguise they wear, Gabriel finally got Embram's undivided attention. "What do you know about something called a Mk. 3A wraith?"

The youth's eyes widened slightly. "Nothing, except that I don't want to even consider its possible existence, let alone talk about it."

Crouching down to stroke the blue-rinse poodle at his feet, skater Embram continued speaking without looking up, his voice suddenly tense. "I have this sinking feeling that you're going to tell me something I don't want to know, Gabriel; and believe me, whatever it is, I don't want to know about it!"

Looking at the snow that was steadily falling outside, the punk Archangel repeated what he had been told by the head of Marcus Enderholt. By the time he had finished, the look on Embram's face reflected the sound of apprehension in his voice.

"Well, that's it, it's over! We might just as well sit here and wait for the end to reach us, and try not to piss our pants when it eventually arrives!"

Picking up the poodle, human Embram sighed and changed the words on the dog's hooded coat to read, 'Repent—For The End Is Gonna Be A Real Bummer.'

"What are you babbling about? Wait for the end to reach us? Are you forgetting who I am and what I'm capable of? This is just another wraith in a long line of wraiths I have dealt with, and I have destroyed countless of their kind over the course of eternity. And believe me, I will do the same to this one!"

"That may have been the case in the past, Gabriel, but there are two major factors which make this situation a little different. The first is the lack of a certain double-edged weapon, and the second concerns a relevant piece of information that you are obviously unaware of."

Placing Fifi back down on the stone floor, Embram smiled for a moment as she pretended not to clean places a dog of her breeding would never be seen cleaning.

"Your friend's information is not complete, I'm afraid."

"He's not my friend, but continue anyway!"

"You see, it concerns the real reason the Mk. 3A was originally designed."

Sitting down on one of the wooden pews, Gabriel looked directly into Embram Ferret Frightener's eyes and said quietly, "What do you mean 'originally de-signed for'? I thought it was all to do with internal security?"

"That was just propaganda: misinformation to keep us on our toes, or cloven hooves, depending on what type of demon you are. No, the real reason for the creation of the Mk. 3A wraith was a military one. A one mission super-soldier, so to speak."

"What? Are you being serious?"

"Yes."

"How come you know all of this?"

Sitting down opposite the angel, Embram let his true form return, his real weight causing a series of creaking protests from the wooden pew.

"In my hatchling days, my grandfather told me about the time he spent working as a security gargoyle in the research and development laboratory and how he had to turn a blind eye when the management held certain illegal parties, if you get my meaning. It was something to do with a holographic, halo fetish group they were all members of ... or at least that's what he told me."

"And?" Although intrigued, Gabriel's instincts told him the narrative had somehow lost its direction. Embram's answer confirmed it.

"And what?"

"And what has that to do with the Mk. 3A wraith?"

"Nothing, it's just a good story."

Normally at this point in a conversation between an Archangel and a minor demon, one of two things would happen. Either the angel in question would blow his divine war horn and commence battle with the foul spawn, or if they knew each other really well, they would probably exchange phone numbers and arrange to do battle via an online internet gaming site (technological progress yet again, I'm afraid). But this particular situation was a little different, and 'different folks mean different strokes', as they say in heaven. (Actually they don't, but on with the story anyway ...)

At first Embram thought the Archangel was crying. He was sitting hunched over, his face buried in his hands, his body rocking backwards and forwards on the pew. Changing back to skater boy, Embram Ferret Frightener sat, slightly embarrassed at the sight of an angel crying and unsure about what to do or say next. Moments later he realised that Gabriel was in fact laughing.

"You're a class one idiot, Embram, do you know that? An innocent fool with about as much brain as an embalmed toad and about as much common sense as that bloody dog of yours! Here we are, you and I, on a mission without equal in all of eternity and with little or no idea what we are really up against! This whole escapade, which started out as a simple 'find and retrieve' operation, is slowly turning into a complete

116

fiasco! I just want to go home, do you know that? Go back and offer my services to the damned committee and be done with it!"

Dropping his hands away from his face, punk Gabriel rested his arms on his knees and stared at his Union Jack *Doc Martens.*

"Maybe you're right, maybe we should just wait for the end to reach us. After all, like you said yourself, we have absolutely no idea what it is we are facing, do we?"

"I didn't actually say that, did I?"

"Sorry?"

"I didn't actually say I knew nothing about the wraith, did I?"

Looking up, Gabriel glared at the youth. "Are you trying to be funny, gargoyle? If you are, I had better warn you that at this particular moment I have no sense of humour whatsoever!"

Now it's fairly safe to say that gargoyles are, in all probability, not the most intelligent of Hell's inhabitants; neither are they creatures of social grace. But if there was one thing this particular gargoyle knew, it was when *not* to push the limited patience of an Archangel too far.

Changing the wording on his own hooded top to 'Be Gentle, I'm A Christian', Embram Ferret Frightener (who still hadn't met a ferret) back-pedalled very quickly.

"What I do know is that the prototype Mk. 3A was to be the first in a limited series of special operation units, all designed specifically to be used in the final battle at Armageddon. They were intended to be the ultimate doomsday weapons, their only purpose to annihilate a certain exclusive target by means of something called a proxy attack."

After an eternity of experiencing everything that life, and the afterlife, had to offer, Archangel Gabriel finally understood just why frustration was such a plague in the mortal realm. As he contemplated starting the final conflict here and now by destroying the gargoyle with his bare human hands, Gabriel rubbed his aching temples and resumed his examination of the *Doc Martens* while Embram continued.

"But as we both now know, ever since the setting up of the two committees and the instigation of the *Joint Policy of Mutual Disarmament* programme, Armageddon has been postponed indefinitely. Because of this, the Mk. 3A programme was shelved."

"OK, so who *was* the original target, and why has the thing suddenly arrived here on this side of the divide?" Gabriel's frustration was growing, and it had just joined forces with impatience.

"The original target was to be *Himself*. Well, your *Himself* that is, not mine."

"What are you talking about? Who is this '*your Himself*'? That doesn't make any ..." Realisation hit the angel squarely between the eyes as the full impact of Embram's words sank in.

"*Him*! You mean *Him,* don't you! They were actually going to try to assassinate *Him?*"

"Well that's the story my grandfather told me, but I have no idea where he got the information from in the first place. All I know is that not long after, he was demoted to demon dung remover, and disappeared in the terrible dung-slide of '86."

Frustration faded from the angel's mind, shock replacing it as a multitude of questions ran through, and around, his celestial brain.

"So if *He* was to be the primary target, why ..."

Gabriel's head suddenly shot up, the red, white and blue Union Jack pattern on his boots no longer of interest as he understood the audacity of such a plan.

"Of course, it's so obvious it's brilliant! *He* would have been the enemy's main target during Armageddon, and thus would have warranted all the protection the army of Heaven could have offered!" Standing up, the Archangel started pacing backwards and forwards in front of Embram, momentarily lost in a battle that had never happened. "The foul Hell spawn from the black pit would have been hard pressed to actually destroy him in a direct attack, but to destroy the *One* via a proxy strike?"

Stopping in mid-stride, the punk Archangel Gabriel nodded and looked back towards Embram. "Ingenious! Absolutely ingenious! What a brilliant piece of military strategy, but who would the surrogate target have been?"

"Ah, right! I think I had better take Fifi out for her allusions: we don't want her to make another mess, do we?"

Quickly standing, Embram had already bent down to pick up the poodle and make a quick exit from the building when a hand grabbed the hood of his top, lifting him bodily into the air. Fifi fell away from his hands, landing with a thump on the stone floor. As he hung there, swinging backwards and forwards, he came face to face with the angry looking angel.

"Firstly, the word you are trying to find is 'ablutions' not 'allusions'; and secondly, I would seriously suggest that you let me in to the little secret you are trying very hard to keep from me!"

Wishing he was hanging about elsewhere at that precise moment, Embram looked down at Fifi and re-signed himself to a painful and ignominious end.

"The Mk. 3A was to be nicknamed."

"And what was that nickname going to be?"

Embram mumbled something as he hung in the air, the words lost as he buried his mouth in the hooded top that now threatened to tear under the strain.

"I didn't hear a word of that, gargoyle! Tell me what the nickname was, or I will ensure your own name will join a very long list I'm compiling for future spiritual disembowelment!"

"It was to be known as the 'Gabe Grinder'."

"What?"

"It was to be nicknamed the 'Gabe Grinder'."

Dropping Ferret Frightener on the floor, just missing a surprised-looking blue-rinse poodle, the stunned Archangel stared into space as his angelic thought processes grappled with the audacity of such a loathsome but simple plan. Then slowly, ever so slowly, a smile grew on Gabriel's face.

"An invisible weapon! An undetectable stealth killer, with only one purpose for its existence! What a brilliant idea! If you can't attack an enemy target directly, then design weapons that will by-pass his defence systems using covert tactics."

His thoughts now totally concentrated on the new revelations running through his mind, Gabriel didn't notice the look of despair growing on Embram's face as the gargoyle-in-human-form stood up and brushed himself down. Picking up the dog, the youth sat back down on the pew and closed his eyes for a brief moment as he tried to regain his composure. Opening them and steadying himself ready for his own personal Armageddon, Embram Ferret Frightener spoke again. "I don't think you quite understand, Gabriel."

"Sorry? what is it that I don't quite understand?" The unexpected statement brought the angel's eyes back to the skater boy, and his thoughts back to the present.

"It pains me to have to tell you this, Gabriel, but you really have no idea what is happening here: no idea at all! If the truth be told, I thought you, of all the heavenly host, would know what was going on as soon as we found out what type of wraith we were dealing with."

Enraged by the audacity of the gargoyle's statement

and the lack of any kind of respect from what, after all, was just a minor demon, the Archangel lost what little patience he may have had left. Reverting to his true form (well actually his *Old Testament* persona, which brought more 'ooohs' and 'aaahs' due to the fashionable fluted gothic armour he wore during that period) and reaching for the terrible *Sword of Retribution,* Archangel Gabriel suddenly felt very stupid when his hand alighted on an empty scabbard.

Seizing the opportunity to save himself from any pain that might be coming his way from one very pissed-off angel of the light, Embram quickly continued. "Look, before we get into the 'And I will smite you, foul demon, and banish your black soulless form back to the deepest pit in Hell' routine, which, by the way, you may find a little difficult without the sword, can we please talk about this like two civilised immortal creatures?"

Feeling more than a little foolish for the first time in a timeless eternity (that is, of course, if you don't count the time he misjudged things while helping Moses with the parting of the Red Sea and realised, too late, that as an Archangel he had never needed to swim before), Gabriel quickly turned back into the punk and tried very hard not to cry. Ignoring the wetness creeping up the leg of his immaculate suit as Fifi decided she wasn't cathedral trained after all, Gabriel sat down again and thought seriously about the revised retirement package recently introduced by the committee.

"OK, Embram, let's just pretend that I have just arrived and you are bringing me up to date with operational progress, shall we? Just what is it I should be aware of, and what relevance does this wraith have to the overall plan?"

Trying hard not to show just how much he was enjoying the new feeling of self-importance he had gained because of the angel's surprising lack of know-ledge concerning the wraith, Embram decided on a dramatic pause before continuing.

The brief silence ended when Fifi broke wind—something else a dog of her calibre should never do.

"If you're asking me if the wraith will try and attack you again, then the answer is no. You see, he has succeeded in his mission and is, in all probability, now inactive."

Looking down at the dog sitting at his feet (who was herself trying to decide which of the other two had farted), Gabriel tried hard to make sense of what he was hearing.

"So you are telling me that the whole purpose of its existence was to cast an annoying but ineffectual spell on me, and then roll over and die?"

"No, that's not what I'm saying, Gabriel! Yes it did cast a spell on you, but that was only the beginning of a very major dilemma you are now facing!"

Standing up, his eyes narrowing as frustration again boiled over into anger, Gabriel screamed, "Listen to me, you worthless piece of gorgon shit! If you don't stop this incessant double talk and start to make sense, I swear I will tear off your bloody head and force that three-headed animal down your neck feet first!"

Realising that his luck was very quickly deserting him, Embram decided that it would be prudent to come to the point more quickly than he had planned.

"*You* were always intended to be the Mk. 3A wraith's initial target, Gabriel, seeing as you are the only member of the heavenly host with unrestricted access to the primary objective. The wraith cast a self-destructing parasite hex on you. A specially designed spell that lies dormant in you until the moment you and your *He* are together. Like I have already said, it was originally designed for the final battle. A foolproof way to ensure a quick and total victory for our side, by eliminating your commander-in-chief and his war-council in one devastating blow."

For a moment Gabriel laughed in total disbelief. Pacing backwards and forwards along the main aisle of the cloisters, the military side of his mind was impressed by the cunning of such a plan. Then, as the full implications of the situation hit him, the Archangel understood for the first time just what real trouble was.

"Wait a minute! That means ..."

Embram watched as Gabriel paused mid-sentence, a look of apprehension beginning to form on his face.

"No, this can't be happening! All of this is impossible! I am the Archangel Gabriel, second only to the *One!* I am the bringer of retribution to all who serve the Dark Lord, and the nemesis of all that is evil! Since the beginning of everything I have been at his side and fought every battle he has commanded me to fight! I am the *Avenging Angel,* and I will smite any ..."

"For everyone's sake, will you just shut up with all that antiquated crap and let me finish?"

The sudden and loud outburst from Embram stopped Gabriel dead in his tracks (well not actually dead, of course, as the only death Gabriel had any personal knowledge of was the one with pink hair), momentarily surprising him as the gargoyle-in-human-form sprang to its feet and walked over to where he was standing open mouthed.

"I'll tell you what it means, shall I? It means that this whole mess is over, and we may as well just sod off back to the other side and face whatever painful punishments the joint committee deem appropriate for two failures like us!"

"What do you mean 'failures'?" Gabriel's eyes registered the gargoyle standing in front of him, but his brain still seemed to be stuck in neutral. "We haven't failed: all we have to do is find *Him* and explain what you and I know is really happening up *there.*"

Looking up at the Archangel, Embram Ferret Frightener shrugged his shoulders and continued in a calmer voice. "It means what it says, Gabriel, F.A.I.L.U.R.E.S! Don't you get it yet? You may be the all-powerful Archangel Gabriel, but at this point that means sweet sod all! You cannot get within spitting distance of your boss without annihilating the pair of you, and just about everything else on both sides of the divide as well!"

For a very brief moment in a timeless void called confusion, Gabriel fought a holy war with his own inner demons. (Sorry about this piece of Victorian melo-drama, but this *is* one of the more dramatic bits of the story, and it *will* sound better in the film version. Trust me!) The stark reality of the gargoyle's words burned deep into his immortal soul as he finally understood what it was to fail. (OK, you can carry on reading now, the boring bit's over!) Sitting back down and kicking out at the poodle, who was now trying out a new trick called 'mount the Archangel's leg', Gabriel beckoned the skater gargoyle to join him.

"Embram, pray sit with me for a while and let us talk of what was, what could have been and what is to be."

"What?"

"Embram, just sit your spotty self down and let's try to sort this frigging mess out!"

Joining Gabriel on the pew and trying hard to ignore Fifi playing 'now mount the gargoyle's leg', Embram waited for the expected revelations to begin.

"Do you know what they used to call me back in the Old Testament days?"

Embram shrugged his shoulders.

"I don't know ... Mr. Archangel maybe?"

"They used to praise me as the prince of fire, and the spirit who presides over thunder and the ripening fruits."

"Nice one! I bet that went down a bomb at parties."

Seemingly ignoring the youth, Gabriel continued.

"And do you know who taught Joseph the seventy languages he spoke at Babel? Or who told old Zacharias that his wife was in the club, and that the child would eventually be known as John the Baptist?"

"Let me guess! ... You?"

"Yes, me!"

Leaning towards Embram, the angel ran his fingers through his red, white and blue hair and sighed.

"And where am I now? I'll tell you where, shall I? I'm up the proverbial creek without a canoe, let alone a paddle. I'm up to my heavenly neck in shit, and I can't find a shovel!"

Embram shifted slightly in his seat and grunted as Gabriel leaned even closer.

"I'm sure you can understand my predicament, Embram. Here I am charged with a task, which, due to unforeseen circumstances, I cannot now complete. I am, in all but a sexual sense, impotent. Are you keeping up with me?"

Now I'm sure that by this point in the story you have realised that Embram Ferret Frightener is a cut above your average demon gargoyle. (A fine example of that old adage: you can lead a gargoyle to water, but sometimes you *can* actually make him think!) Well, this may be true, but sitting next to an Archangel who, in a bad light, looks not too dissimilar to Johnny Rotten, and whose incessant ramblings seemed to be leading absolutely nowhere, can be a little more than unnerving, to say the least! Feeling even more uncomfortable as Gabriel slipped an arm around his thin shoulders, Embram the skater boy thought about his mother's warning about talking to strange angels (and this angel was definitely starting to act strange) and tried to edge his way back along the pew.

He failed, Gabriel's arm tightening its grip on his shoulders as he carried on with his monologue. "You see, my new friend ... we are friends now, aren't we? Yes, of course we are. You see, my friend, we can't abandon the mission after all, can we? If we do fail, as you seem to think we already have, what will be left in either of our opposing camps? Nothing, that's what will be left, nothing! The committees will merge both realms into one conglomerate, and what will you and I have? We will have total chaos, that's what. No defined barriers between good and evil, no more 'fight the good fight,' no more inter-realm darts matches and definitely no canine companion for you, my scaly friend!"

Finally pulling away from the angelic embrace, Embram quickly moved to the other end of the pew and looked at Gabriel through narrowing eyes.

"Something tells me that you are dreaming up a plan which I am not going to appreciate, and that same something also makes me worried; very worried indeed!"

Hurriedly standing up as the Archangel moved along the pew towards him, Embram Ferret Frightener (who at this point wanted to be anything but a transformed gargoyle on what was turning out to be a suicide mission) picked up the dog and edged away from where the Archangel now sat smiling.

"Whatever it is, Gabriel, the answer is no! I'm just going to call home and arrange to be picked up. The committee will understand the final impossibility of the mission, and the role *He* had in disrupting it using the wraith. I'm sure they will find another way to ..."

He suddenly found he couldn't speak any more, the neck of the hooded top yet again forcing its way into his mouth as Gabriel appeared in front of him.

"*He?* Who is this *He*, and what has any of this got to do with the mission, or the wraith?" Gabriel's voice blasted through the cathedral as he drew Embram's face near to his own, his eyes glowing red as anger built inside him. As their faces drew closer together, Gabriel's voice lowered to a whisper. "What is it you haven't told me, you useless worm? What else have you decided to hide from me ... and why?"

Pulling Embram even closer, until their noses touched, Gabriel tightened his grip on the hood and glared at the youth. "Make sure you understand what I'm about to say, as there will be no second chance before I tear you apart! I'm going to drop you back onto the floor, and when I do you had better be forthcoming with a very good explanation! A very good explanation indeed, if you wish to forgo a great deal of pain and bad luck for the next dozen or so millennia!"

Hitting the cold floor with a resounding bump, skater Embram's own temper started to build as he looked at the Archangel standing over him. Pushing away the face-licking poodle, the boy stood, picked up his skateboard and glared defiantly at the Archangel.

"Who do you think *He* is? *He* is my *He!* The Fallen One! The Dark Angel of Oblivion! The Lord of the Darkness! Who do you think originally designed the Mk. 3A? Exactly who do you think invented the parasite spell in the first place? And who do you think is the only one with the authority to activate the wraith? As soon as you told me about the wraith I knew we were finished and the mission was over, and it then became obvious why my *He* is also missing. My *He* has planned all of this, knowing that the committee could only send *you* to find your *He!* Don't you see the irony in all of this, Gabriel? This is the perfect opportunity for my *Him* to gain it all without all the hassle and expense of Armageddon! All my *He* has to do is sit back in some quiet corner and wait for you to do the job for him. Then, when it's all over, he will suddenly reappear with some excuse about a satanic nervous breakdown and simply take it all! Like I said, it's over Gabriel, we can't win! You can't get near to your *Him,* let alone take him back. So, in essence, the committee has succeeded. On the other hand, if you do approach your *Him,* neither of you will survive to stop 'Mr. Horns and Tail' doing whatever he wants!"

Pointing to the smaller skateboard, Embram watched as the blue-rinse poodle in designer shades climbed on and waited for him to join her. Dropping his own board onto the stone floor, he was about to step on when Gabriel's voice stopped him.

"You're right, Embram; for the first time in my existence I am totally powerless and without use." (Actually that's also not true; he and Archangel Raphael were nearly caught in an embarrassing situation in Sodom just before its demise. They had gone there to 'cast wrath and terror from above' prior to *His* arrival, but had been distracted by Persian wine and a certain young woman of ill repute called Delilah.)

Positive he had misheard, Embram climbed on to the board, pushing off with one foot as he and Fifi headed towards the exit. When Gabriel's next words reached him the skater gargoyle very nearly fell off in surprise.

"OK, I'll say it, Embram! I need your help ... *Please!"*

Spinning the skateboard round, he jumped off and looked at the angel.

"Pretty please, dude?"

Walking up to Embram, Archangel Gabriel looked down and grinned.

"Don't push it, Embram, there's a good demon!"

Leaning against the stone wall, Embram examined a dirty fingernail and watched in amusement as Fifi adjusted her sunglasses and ran her skateboard head-long into a closed oak door.

"OK, Embram, take this as the only warning you will be getting! Whatever you do from this point on, do not in any way, shape or form try to take advantage of my temporarily problematic position. Is that clear? Very well then, I'm asking you what your thoughts are concerning our mutual problem. And yes, I'm open to any ideas that you may have to help improve our situation."

Smiling to himself as he watched the blue-rinse canine grow two more heads and devour the offending door, skater boy Embram shrugged his thin shoulders and chewed on the dirty nail.

"How devious is this cherub?"

" 'Devious'? What do you mean 'devious'? He may well be a total shit, but he is still a member of the heavenly host."

Yeah, sure, whatever! You, Mr. Archangel, you are also part of the same pack, are you not? And you're about as devious as it comes when you need to be!"

Three loud belches from the direction of the three-headed poodle brought another smile to the lips of the youth as he continued. "So, like I said, how devious is this Marcus Enderholt when he needs to be? And just how much control do you really have over him?"

To his horror, Gabriel realised that he was actually starting to admire this lesser demon. He made a mental note to visit the confessional when all of this was finally over.

"In answer to your first question, I should imagine Enderholt is very devious indeed. After all, he is the head of a union that is well known in Heaven for its unopposed political successes. And he does have this uncanny knack of knowing a lot of confidential information concerning certain things he should have absolutely no knowledge of at all. As far as your second question is concerned my spotty friend; well, that's an easy one to answer: I have total control over cherub Marcus Enderholt the Third, just as I have over every other member of the immaculate host."

Ignoring the obvious conceit in the angel's voice, Embram Ferret Frightener re-grew the dirty fingernail and walked over to where a now single-headed poodle was sitting contemplating the possibility of eating another wooden door.

"OK, so use your influence on the cherub. Get him to tap into the wraith's virtual line and find out what numbers are listed in its phone book. At least that way we can find out who, or what, we may be up against."

Inwardly cursing himself for not thinking of something so simple, Gabriel dialled Marcus Enderholt's virtual number and nodded to Embram when the ringing tone told him a connection had been made.

CHAPTER SIXTEEN

"Damn it, Gabriel! Answer your phone will you! Why is it that every time I call your bloody answer-phone is on?"

The shrunken head of Marcus Enderholt the Third (OK, just for you: Randy to his friends) tried for the third time to re-establish contact with the angel on his virtual phone. His mind was fixed firmly on his need to breathe while on this side of the divide and the pressing problem of the dwindling supply of air at his present location.

He was still unsure what had actually happened. One moment he had been hanging from a chain attached to the ear of the Archangel and the next he had found himself transported towards a strange looking creature with no dress sense and hair whiter than his own. It wasn't until he had arrived in the smelly darkness that he realised just where he was. Marcus knew it was a wraith the instant he materialised inside the pocket of the red racing leathers; the overpowering smell of corruptness a tell-tale sign that he was somewhere he definitely shouldn't have been. (Actually corruptness is quite a rare smell these days, due in no small part to the Dark Committee's introduction of the *Hades Clean Air Act,* and the subsequent redundancy of at least a third of the fart demon workforce.) But it was the patent stamp, embossed on the smooth leather of the pocket, that brought home to him just how much shit now covered him. Looking around his temporary prison, the shrunken head of the cherub examined his limited options. Finding he had none, he resigned himself to a fate far, far worse than an eternity as an Archangel's night-light.

Realising just what that particular fate might entail at the hands of a wraith, Marcus Enderholt the Third (in his present state, literally the *head* of Heaven's largest union) spent 2.3 seconds watching his immortal life pass before his eyes and cursed Gabriel for placing him in this position in the first place. Suddenly wishing he had a mother to say goodbye to, the cherub started to hold his breath.

As his surroundings started to swim, his eyes rolling upwards in their sockets as asphyxiation took hold, Marcus Enderholt the Third smiled as he heard the far off chimes of heavenly bells. He was going home, one way or another.

As his answer-phone automatically engaged, the voice of his personal nemesis brought a sudden exhalation of breath from Enderholt's mouth.

"About f***ing time, Marcus! What in *His* name have you been doing? I have urgent need of your questionable talents to perform a small but important task for me!"

Waiting for the spinning to stop, the head of the cherub fought hard to control the anger that bubbled away just beneath the surface. Fought and lost.

"Oh! So you have finally decided to answer my calls, have you? Well I am *so* pleased you could spare some of your valuable time to remember that I exist, in mind if not in body! So what is it that I, a humble nothingness, can do for the high and mighty Archangel bloody Gabriel?"

Ignoring the outburst for now, Gabriel brought Enderholt up to date on the situation, pausing for dramatic effect before informing the head of its assignment. The response was both immediate and expected.

"You are taking the mortal piss, aren't you? Here I

am, trapped in the pocket of a wraith whose power is without equal in any area of Heaven or Hell, and you want me to do what?"

"What I want is for you to tap into its virtual phone book and call all the numbers you find listed there! It really is that simple, Marcus; nothing too difficult or strenuous ... or shall I just conveniently forget about a certain body walking around without a head?"

Winking at a puzzled Embram, Gabriel waited as the expected silence momentarily halted the conversation, his smile eventually broadening as the voice of the cherub returned briefly.

"I'll call you back!"

As the line went dead, Gabriel looked at his watch, which now read 9:30am, and then over to where snow was drifting in through a doorway without a door. Thinking 'change of clothes', and replacing the pristine suit with a pair of designer jeans, white *Ben Sherman* shirt and a 1960's fish-tail parka, he pulled up the fur-lined hood and made his way out of the cathedral.

"And by the way, Embram, I've decided on a small change of plan. If *I* can't get near to *my* main man, then someone else is going to have to do it for me."

Skateboarding past the Archangel and out into the snow-covered cathedral grounds, the human form of Embram, now clad in a fluorescent yellow ski-suit (followed by Fifi, resplendent in a shocking-pink dog suit with the words 'Barbie Ate My Hamster' emblazoned across it), shook his head.

"No way, dude! No way is *that* someone going to be me! You can use smoke signals for all I care, just don't even think of asking me to do it!"

As the two boarders disappeared from view, Gabriel smiled and spoke quietly to himself. "Of course not, Embram. As if I would even consider it ..."

CHAPTER SEVENTEEN

"Oh, how I love Sunday mornings! No shop to open, no having to go in that tin box on wheels you insist on driving, and, most of all, no pampering those miserable wretches and their pathetic fixations! Without a doubt, Gerald, Sundays have turned out to be one of your better ideas."

Draining the last of the coffee from a mug inscribed 'Better The Devil You Know', and adorned with a cartoon of Kylie Minogue, complete with horns, a tail and very little else, Samuel Nevis turned the page of the newspaper propped up against the toast-rack in front of him. He smiled as he read the latest opinion poll concerning the continuing fall in church attendances. "But, most of all, I like the way you arranged to have Sundays placed at the end of the weekly period, and the nice touch of having every Sunday dedicated to me."

Looking up from his copy of *Starfleet Herald* (a newspaper he thought should be published, so obviously if he thought it should be, then it was) Gerald Oliver Davies looked at his friend sitting at the breakfast table opposite him.

"Pardon me? What do you mean 'dedicated to you'?"

"Sundays. It was a touching gesture having every Sunday dedicated to me by making each one a Sabbat day."

Shaking his head in amusement, Gerald adjusted his Captain Kirk face and picked up another slice of toast.

"It's *Sabbath*, Samuel. Sundays are *Sabbath* days, and in any case today is Saturday."

"Sabbat? Sabbath? What's in a name? And who cares what they're called, it was still a nice gesture on your part and I do appreciate the thought, Gerald."

Turning the page of his paper, Samuel scanned an article entitled 'Aliens Abducted My Mother's Dog', and dialled a number on his virtual phone. As his call went unanswered, he smiled and looked up again.

"Oh, and by the way, today *is* Sunday ... I decided we would give Saturday a miss this week, if that's OK with you?"

Returning his attention to his own paper, Gerald smiled and blinked twice in quick succession; an audible groan of disappointment coming from across the table as the kitchen faded, instantaneously being replaced by the interior of the Ford Sierra. As the car pulled into the small car park behind the shop, Samuel folded his newspaper, ate the last piece of toast and shook his head before opening the passenger door and climbing out.

"You really are a killjoy, Gerald, do you know that? No wonder the puritans loved you so much ... all work and no time off for good, or bad, behaviour!"

Standing beside the vehicle and watching as his colleague gathered his scattered belongings from the back seat, Science Officer Lucifer Spock said quietly to himself, "Come back Bacchus, all really *is* forgiven!"

He was about to close the passenger door when the virtual phone rang inside his head. Answering the call, he thought 'Science Officer Spock, *Star Trek IV: The Voyage Home'*, and allowed the instantaneous transformation to take effect while the connection was made. Following Captain Kirk through the car park and up to the rear of the shop, he was about to enter when someone he didn't recognise (but speaking from a phone number he was all too well acquainted with) spoke in his head:

"Hello! Who is it I am talking to, please?"

Switching over to answer-phone, Samuel waited as the pre-recorded message ran its course. 'Hello and welcome to the *Hades Automated Answering Service*. We are very sorry, but his greatness Lord Lucifer, Ruler of the Underworld, Spirit of Eternal Wickedness and president of the Styx Tropical Freshwater Fish Society is not available at the moment. If you wish to leave a message, please speak after the scream …'

After a very brief silence the caller hung up.

CHAPTER EIGHTEEN

The usual crowds of Saturday shoppers packed the busy High Street as the three walked through the steadily falling snow, heading towards the relative quietness of a nearby coffee shop. Reaching the glass-fronted building, Embram discreetly dismissed both skateboards from existence, thought 'dog lead,' and apologising profusely bent down and tied a very indignant Fifi to a nearby bench.

"I'm sorry about this Fifi, but we don't make the rules here." He spoke in a whisper as he stroked her curly blue fur. "I know this is embarrassing for you, but please try to understand my predicament."

A firm hand gripping his shoulder brought his head around.

"Will you *stop* talking to that damned animal and get inside! We still have a number of major problems to sort out and the more we fart about, the less time we are going to have to deal with them! So move it, will you?"

Sneaking a final hug (an act which told him that three-headed hell-hounds, on this side of the divide at least, need to be washed occasionally ... even ones of Fifi's impeccable breeding), Embram straightened and reluctantly followed Gabriel into the warmth of the shop. They had just sat down at an empty table when they were approached by a bored-looking waitress. Without bothering to look at them, she sniffed loudly and reeled off the menu in a well-practised monotone, much to the annoyance of the Archangel.

"We have Cappuccino, Latte, Kenyan, Nicaraguan, Costa Rican, Indian, and Brazilian. You can have coffee with cream, with milk or black, vegetarian coffee ..."

"Do you by any slim chance have any Tibetan dark bean with yaks' milk?"

Looking at the punk in the parka, who had done the unforgivable in interrupting her verbal flow, Sharon Williams (as was the name printed on the plastic badge pinned to her blouse) deliberately failed to force back a sarcastic remark and smiled her best 'of course the customer is always right ... I don't think' smile.

"No, sir, I'm afraid not. Seeing as we don't get the Dalai Lama in here very often, there is no real call for it, is there? And anyway, we seem to have run out of yaks' milk, so the answer is a double no, I suppose!"

It was the spotty youth who spoke next, as Embram attempted to diffuse a situation that, through experience, he knew could only end in excruciating pain for Miss Williams at the hands of an extremely annoyed Archangel.

"Just two coffees, made from coffee beans, will do fine thank you, miss; and could you please make one decaffeinated?"

Looking down her nose at them, the woman shrugged her shoulders and scribbled illegibly on her pad as she turned and walked away. Glaring across the table to where Embram was sitting, Gabriel made a mental note concerning his personal future involvement in Miss Williams' afterlife and frowned at the ski-suited skater boy.

"Decaffeinated coffee? Since when have you ever had decaffeinated *anything* where you come from?"

"I haven't, I just like the word decaffeinated. It sounds so much like decapitated, doesn't it?"

Reaching for the sword that wasn't there, Gabriel's frown deepened as he spoke again. "Yes it does, you idiot, and I agree decapitated itself is a wonderful word; but one I like even more when it's combined with the words 'gargoyle's' and 'head'!"

Leaning back in his seat, the Archangel unzipped his parka and thrust both hands in to the pockets as he looked at his companion sitting opposite him. "Enough of this friendly repartee, Embram, let's just get back to the situation in hand, shall we? It seems that *we* have a slight problem, and it's a problem that needs us to perform a radical re-examination of our options before we continue."

"No, Gabriel, it's *you* who has the problem! As you are so fond of reminding me, I'm just a minor demon from an unimportant part of Hell, so why should I worry if we get them back or not? Where I come from, it will make little or no difference who, or what, holds the power: the Committee or the Dark One, it's all much the same really. Life and the afterlife will still be one long grind for both the dead and those of us who work there. So, you give me one good reason why I shouldn't just leave now and return to what I've always known!"

"Only *one* reason, gargoyle? Well, how about I tell a certain all-time winner of the ancient Greek *Twelve Labours Tournament* that you have a certain something that belongs to him? A something that I'm sure he would like back, but without a blue-rinse and preferably with more than one head."

Snorting steam through his human nostrils (which hurt even more than it usually did through his gargoyle ones), skater Embram narrowed his eyes as he leaned forward over the table.

"You are a total bastard, Gabriel! A class one shit, without an ounce of real pity or understanding! You know Fifi is the only good thing that has ever happened to me in all of my miserable existence, but you would still make sure she was taken from me, wouldn't you?"

"You had better believe it, Embram! I have spent all of *my* existence serving *Him*, and ensuring that the status quo is preserved; and I'm not going to stop now! *He* has his faults and idiosyncrasies, I know, and this *Star Trek* thing is one of the most annoying, but above all else he is still the *One*, and that is something that will *never* change as far as I'm concerned. He is my Commander in Chief, my boss, and, I hope, my friend, and I would sacrifice my own existence for him if necessary."

Resting his elbows on the table and his face in his hands, Embram sighed and looked Gabriel straight in the eye. "Do you know what the *real* problem is?"

"No, but I'm sure you are going to enlighten me."

"The real problem is that you have never failed at anything, have you Gabriel? Everything you do is done to one point past perfection every time, and then it's done to one point past even that. You have no idea what it's like to continually worry, to panic just in case you've cocked things up, yet again! Well, this time not only have you failed, you have failed big time; and because of that, it's all over! Face it, Gabriel, there is no longer a mission to complete, so there is absolutely no ..."

Pausing as the waitress with attitude placed two steaming cups of coffee and the bill on to the table in front of them, Embram smiled and waited for her attention to be diverted to another table before continuing. "... no point in wasting any more time on this, seeing as there is *no way* you can carry out the most crucial part of the task, is there?"

Picking up the nearer cup, Embram drank and decided that he didn't like decaffeinated after all.

"Yes, you could tell Hercules about Fifi; and yes, he could take her back, but the unalterable fact that you have failed will still remain." Not taking his eyes off the Archangel, Embram drained the last of the coffee, grimaced, and decided that maybe he should have kept his mouth shut. But it was too late now, so what the hell! (I know, I know! You're thinking to yourself, "what is it with this melodramatic prose rubbish again?" Well, as I said before, it will sound better in the film version ... believe me, I am an author of sorts.)

"I know what scheme you're planning, Gabriel. I know it's one that concerns me doing your part of the mission for you, isn't it? When we find your *Him,* you want me to be *you*, and get *Him* to return with us, don't you? Now that's a *wonderful* idea, isn't it? Can you honestly see me, a foul demon from the dark underworld, asking the divine one if he could just 'pop home and sort out a few problems'? I can just imagine it now, can't you? There will be quite a lot of the 'O foul devil spawn from Hell, thou shalt no longer cause suffering or torment upon any living thing' stuff, and a great deal of excruciating pain for yours truly as *He* spiritually castrates me! I'm sorry, Gabriel, but the answer is no, and it's going to remain no until Hell freezes over! There is nothing you or anyone else can offer me that will make me want to carry out such a task! Nothing! Do you understand me? Nothing!"

Leaning his head to one side, Gabriel smiled slightly and said quietly, "Nothing, Embram? Are you sure about that? How about your very own soul?"

CHAPTER NINETEEN

As usual, the queue already stretched past the three adjacent shops by the time they had changed the door sign from 'closed' to 'open', the growing mass of uniformed Trekkies waiting patiently for their personal Heaven to open its gate.

Not bothering to hide the look of boredom that was remodelling his Spock look-alike face, Samuel Nevis watched as the first of them entered the shop and made her way directly to the counter.

"Have you a copy of this month's *Disembowelling Barbie* magazine?"

The bored expression turned to a smile as he leaned on the counter and looked at the teenage girl. The long purple hair, deathly white face, black eye shadow and green lipstick all complimented the scarlet mock-Victorian corset and ankle length skirt she was wearing. Ignoring the dozen or so other customers who now filled the shop, Lucifer Spock walked round the counter and stood facing the girl.

"I must admit, the outfit is very fetching for a succubus, but there's just one small thing ... your tail's showing."

Quickly glancing at the floor behind her, the young Goth groaned and amended her disguise before leaning closer to him and whispering, "Sorry about that, Almighty Dark Lord of the Foulest Pit, I will ensure that such a mistake does not happen again."

Shaking his head and letting the smile grow a little,

Samuel looked around the shop and then returned his attention to the girl.

"He's gone for the sandwiches, so we have a few minutes. What news do you have for me ... and let's dispense with the usual formalities, shall we? Just plain 'Mr. Nevis' will do at this present time."

Leaning even closer, the female demon whispered into his pointed ear, her forked tongue darting in and out as she forced back an urge to see what he tasted like. "It is done O Mighty ... sorry, I mean Mr. Nevis. The spell has been cast, and the demon slayer Gabriel is no longer of any consequence to us."

"Good! That pleases me. And for that you should be *very* grateful, but what about the *thing* with him? Does it know what is to be done?"

Suddenly looking distinctly uneasy, the Goth succubus moved away slightly before answering, her dark green eyes trying hard to look anywhere but into his. "Well, not exactly. You see, there's been a little bit of a mix up ..."

" 'Mix up'? Just what sort of a 'mix up' are we talking about here?"

The room froze in time as Samuel blinked twice, his Spock persona falling away as he reached out and grasped the Goth demon with a well manicured hand, lifting the creature high above his head. (A head which, like the rest of his true form, differed very little from that of the Vulcan whose outward appearance he had taken on.) Glaring through glowing red eyes, his menacing voice was now a guttural growl as he spoke through a mass of razor sharp teeth. "So? I'm waiting! What is it you have to tell me?"

Looking down from her elevated position, the succubus (whose given name, incidentally, was Nickalastic ... but that's another story for another time) fought hard not to panic as she faced almost certain oblivion. She failed miserably.

"It's … it's really not my fault, your Darkness, I'm just the messenger! It seems that an unfortunate mistake was made during the processing of your orders and due to this Ebernam Throat Ripper was not, after all, ordered to accompany the Archangel on the mission … sorry."

Bringing the demon's terrified face closer to his own, Samuel (now complete with horns and a tail of his own) spoke slowly, his breath singeing her eyebrows and turning the iridescent purple hair white. "So in that case, who *is* representing my interests here?"

"I believe its appointed name is Embram Ferret Frightener, my Dark Lord. It is, so I'm told, a very minor gargoyle, employed as an operative at one of your arrival points. An irrelevant and worthless creature, with little or no knowledge of anything outside of its miserable existence, and consequently of no threat to your overall plan, I'm sure."

"No threat you say?" Licking the Goth succubus's face with a trio of forked tongues, Lucifer (no longer) Spock cocked his head to one side and allowed a look of understanding to momentarily come to rest on his face.

"Just an irrelevant and worthless creature, is it? I see, but I believe that there may be just one small point you seem to be overlooking in your assessment of the situation!" The look of understanding disappeared as Samuel tightened his grip on the female demon. "As well as being *irrelevant*, this creature also has no idea whatsoever about any of this, does it? As far as the gargoyle is concerned, it is looking for me! Acting on orders from the committee to find me and persuade me to return! Because of this, the creature is a very serious threat to the final outcome of my plan!"

By way of a scientific explanation of what happened next, imagine a condom blown up to its maximum extent, tied to a heavy weight, and dropped into the ocean just off the coast of Cornwall. (Why Cornwall, you ask? Simple: it's a lovely place!) What happens when it reaches a great depth? The answer is that it implodes due to the increasing pressure of the water that surrounds it. With this in mind, picture a female Goth, complete with tail, held at arm's length and expanding rapidly until she resembles a grotesque fairground balloon floating near the ceiling of the shop "I know you're only the messenger, my sweet little succubus, and because of that small fact I shouldn't take my frustration out on you. But then again you do see my predicament, don't you?"

Changing back to the Vulcan science officer, Nevis drew back his arm and looked intently at the Goth with a tail now floating above him, the smile returning to his face as he thought the word 'pin'. Transferring his gaze to the shiny metal object he now held, and then back to the terrified face of the expanded demon, Lucifer Spock shrugged his uniformed shoulders, grinned, and thrust his hand upwards. The sound of the exploding succubus was accompanied by a noise not dissimilar to a loud belch as the room returned to normal, the tattered remnants of the demon dissolving in mid-air before reaching the crowded floor. Adjusting his Spock face slightly, Samuel Nevis surveyed the re-animated shop and considered for a moment the nature of the information the succubus had brought. If the phone call he had received earlier was also connected to the new situation, the problem could be more serious than he at first thought. Whoever it was had called him was, he was sure, part and parcel of the new and annoying changes in his well-laid plan. A plan that could not, and would not, be changed under any circumstances. Even if things *were* changing on the battlefield, his overall war plan would not.

As James T. Kirk entered the shop carrying lunch, Lucifer Spock smiled his best pseudo-smile and served the nearest spotty customer.

CHAPTER TWENTY

Embram sat staring into the empty coffee cup as Gabriel made a virtual phone call, the offer he had been made temporarily delaying any thought of abandoning the Archangel or the mission. Could Gabriel actually do it? Did he *really* have the divine clout within the heavenly ranks to arrange such an unheard of thing? Shifting his gaze to the Archangel, he waited until the phone conversation had ended before speaking.

"If I do say 'yes' to whatever new plan you're hatching, and understand I'm *not* committing myself in any way at the moment, can you *really* deliver on your offer?"

Looking at the bill lying on the table between them, the punk angel sighed and shook his head slowly. "Just look at that, will you? £3.50 for two cups of instant coffee! You would think they would at least serve it in a cafetière for that price!"

Dropping his head hard onto the table in frustration, Embram stared at the stained wooden surface, picked up the bill and ate it.

"OK! OK! I'll do whatever it takes to bring an end to this damned mission! All I want is to get back to a normal life, as far away from you as possible. So just tell me your bloody plan, and let's get on and do it!" Lifting his head and spitting out what was left of the paper, skater Embram frowned as he saw the broad smile on the angel's face.

"That's better, my ugly friend! You know it's all for the best in the long run."

Standing, Archangel Gabriel reached into the pocket of the parka, brought out four gold-coloured coins, and placed them next to the two empty cups.

"You're actually going to pay?" Embram gave Gabriel a puzzled look as he also prepared to leave. "Well this *has* to be a first ... but why?"

Walking towards the door, Gabriel answered without turning, "I hate chocolate money!"

He had spiritually wet himself when the answer-phone identified the number he had dialled; the cramped confines of the wraith's pocket suddenly closing in on him as his self-control decided enough was enough and deserted what was left of Marcus Enderholt the Third. (No friends = no Randy.) Since ending the call he had sat in the pocket (we are back to semantics again here, are we not? It seems we have to define whether or not a head can actually *sit*, or is it just a figure of speech? The answer, after much thought and deliberation is ... who really cares?) and pondered on the now very distinct possibility of spending the rest of eternity nodding in the rear window of Lucifer's limousine. When his virtual phone suddenly rang the spiritual wetness returned.

"Well, Enderholt, any news for me?"

For the one and only time in his celestial existence he was pleased to hear Gabriel's voice on the other end of the line, but that didn't stop the fear boiling over into anger as he answered.

"Do you f***ing know whose answer-phone I have just called? Have you any god-forsaken idea who I very nearly spoke to?"

"Enderholt will you stop blaspheming and calm down, please? Take a deep breath and start again before you hyperventilate."

"Calm down? You're telling me to calm down?"

"Marcus! You're shouting at me again. Remember what happened last time you forgot yourself and raised your voice to yours truly?"

A vivid picture of wax candles slipped into the thought processes in Marcus Enderholt's head, forcing him to shut the runaway mouth before any more verbal damage could be done.

"That's better, Marcus. And now I have your attention again, tell me the outcome of the little task I set you. Whose numbers did you find in the wraith's phone book?"

"There was just the *one* number!" Marcus Enderholt's voice was quieter, but an undercurrent of anger was still evident as he spoke. "And do you *know* who that phone number belonged to, Gabriel? Have you any idea who I nearly spoke to?"

"Now let me have a guess at this one, Marcus. Would it by any slim chance have been Master Dark Lord Lucifer himself?" The obvious chuckle in the Arch-angel's voice brought the cherub's anger flooding back with a vengeance.

"You knew, didn't you? You knew all along whose number I would find, but you still made me call! Well that's it! I'm finished with you and your stupid damn mission! You can go and take a running jump for all ..."

"Just one small point, Marcus, before you burn all your river crossings and find yourself stranded in the shite, so to speak."

"And what point might that be, you winged wanker?"

"If I do take a *running jump*, as you so eloquently suggest, who will be left to rescue you from an eternity stuck in the pocket of a de-activated wraith?"

The realisation that once again Gabriel had won the moment was evident in the lack of any verbal response from the head. Pausing for a few brief seconds, the Archangel savoured the victory, then continued. "I ...

we, may not be able to sense this particular wraith, but *you* are another matter. I can sense that you are not that far away. I suggest you *sit*, or *lay*, very still and we will be along shortly."

Marcus Enderholt was contemplating the possible consequences of a sarcastic response when Gabriel unexpectedly spoke again. "And by the way, Enderholt, just one small thing for you to think about while you are awaiting our arrival ... I *will* want to know exactly what a wanker is when we next meet."

CHAPTER TWENTY ONE

It was Gabriel who noticed first as they left the coffee shop, his eyes drawn to the dog lead still tied to the wooden bench, but minus a dog.

"I have a little good news and a lot of bad news for you, Embram," he said, looking at the space where the dog had been. "It looks like someone's taken a fancy to your blue furry friend, but on the bright side at least they've left the lead."

Zipping up the ski-suit (which was now lime-green, with matching yeti boots), skater Embram looked past the angel, grinned, and carried on walking.

"No worries, dude, we'll find her easy enough."

Choosing to ignore the continuing references to his so-called street credibility, Gabriel pulled up the fur-lined hood of the parka against the steadily falling snow, thrust his hands into the pockets and caught up with the teenager.

"This may seem a stupid question, gargoyle, but just *how* are we going to find her?"

"Simple, my main man, we just wait for the scream."

Gabriel was about to ask the inevitable question, when from a nearby side street a scream rang out.

"There! Told you we would find her, didn't I?"

His eyes following the path of Embram's outstretched finger, Gabriel couldn't help but smile at the sight that greeted him. Trotting out of the whiteness of the snow storm, plainly ignoring the curses from shoppers who had to weave their way around her, Fifi Lamoure appeared, her small mouth holding on to the ragged remnants of a pair of faded denim jeans. Stopping at the feet of the Archangel, she dropped the tattered material, sat down, and raised one paw. Bending down and picking up the torn portion of clothing, Gabriel looked at the dog, smiled and whispered, "I bet you gave whoever it was a surprise or two ... or three."

Throwing the shredded fabric into a rubbish bin, Gabriel waited as Embram picked up the animal, then motioned towards the rapidly emptying street ahead of them.

"We have a new plan to devise, Embram, and very little time left to carry it out, so I suggest that we find a dry place and prepare ourselves for what is to come."

"But what about ... you know, the head thing? Shouldn't we at least try to find it?"

Putting on his best 'Ah yes, I almost forgot about him' look, Gabriel grinned and shook his head.

"No need. I know exactly where Master Enderholt is, and I also know how to get him back. Will you ever get to grips with what I can do, Embram? It would pay for you to remember the calibre of the divine being you are teamed up with, and just how good this particular angel is. In *all* areas!"

Blinking once and ignoring the tirade of insults that suddenly began to stream into his left ear, Gabriel flicked at the newly-returned cherub-head earring and started to walk along the snow-covered street. By the time they reached the steps of the *White House Hotel* the storm had become a blizzard and the streets were deserted.

"This one will do." Gabriel's voice was muffled behind the fur-lined hood of the parka. He stood back and examined the building. "We will only want the room for one night. Let's be as inconspicuous as possible, shall we Embram?"

"Why?" Embram the skater gargoyle had also stepped back and was trying hard to see just what the angel found so interesting in a plain brick building.

"What do you mean *why?* The last thing we want is a spotty youth and his blue poodle drawing attention to us!"

"No, Gabriel, *why* do we need a room is what I mean. Isn't all of this a bit pointless seeing as none of us can feel the cold anyway? Why don't we just find an empty bench and do our planning there?"

Focussing his attention once again on his teenage companion, Gabriel pulled back the hood of the parka and motioned towards the steps leading up to a re-volving glass door.

"Because, you simple minded creature, in *there* we will be just two more mortals sheltering from the storm! In any case, how is it that something from one of the boiling tar pits of Hell can stand cold like this? This must be your worst nightmare, freezing your balls off in weather like this."

Walking past the Archangel and up to the door, Embram waited for Fifi to join him, then pushed at one of the large glass panels.

"And you call *me* simple minded? Firstly, we don't have tar pits where I work, and secondly, Mr. High and Mighty, gargoyles don't have balls."

Not waiting for a reply, Embram unzipped the green ski-suit, thought 'change' and stepped into the revolving doorway. Entering the empty hotel lobby, Robbie Williams and his pet blue-rinse poodle walked up to the desk and grinned broadly at the shocked receptionist.

"Hi there, my name is …"

He was interrupted by a voice from behind him.

"*His* name is Robbie Smith and I'm Liam Brown. We are part of the famous *Brit-Pop Impressionists* show, soon to be performing at a venue near here."

Ignoring the confused look on the young woman's

face, Embram turned towards one half of the Gallagher brothers and started to speak. Gabriel stopped him.

"Just book us both in will you, Mr. Smith, and then can we *please* get on with the task in hand?"

Shrugging his shoulders, Embram picked up a pen from the desk and filled in two of the hotel's reception cards. Still stunned, the receptionist took them and checked the details.

"Will you both be paying by credit card Mr. ..." the woman looked at the cards and then back to the two figures standing in front of her, "Mr. Embram Ferret Frightener and the Archangel Gabriel? I'm sorry, I don't quite understand. Is this some kind of joke? I thought you said your names were ..."

Pushing Robbie Smith to one side, Liam Brown leaned over the desk, blew gently into the receptionist's face and whispered softly into her ear, "You will give me the keys to an empty room and from that point on you will have no memory of us ever being here." Taking the key with a tag marked 'Room 86' that she held out for him, Gabriel turned, grabbed Embram by the arm and marched him towards the stairs.

"When we get to the room, you *will* change back and you *will* do as I say from now on! If not, I promise you that your head *will* join Enderholt's! Is that perfectly clear?"

Thinking 'change' again, skater boy Embram grabbed the keys from the angel's hand, picked up the poodle and ran up the stairs two at a time.

"Yeah, whatever dude. But just remember, without me you and your plan are history, so maybe you should start being nice to me from now on."

Watching the boy and his dog disappear round a bend in the stairs, Gabriel closed his eyes for a moment and remembered the good old days. Slaying demons had been easy compared to working with these two. And let's be straight here, shall we: working

153

with a gargoyle and a hell-hound was something he would never have considered a possibility in the past. Looking around the empty lobby, Gabriel changed his appearance back to that of the punk mod, sighed, and followed Embram up the stairs. As he slowly climbed towards the second floor, a new emotion suddenly popped into his already weary mind, smiled, and introduced itself. "Hi there, Mr. Gabriel, I'm your new friend despair, and I'm here to *really* piss you off, seeing as things are somewhat cocked up, it seems!" Suddenly feeling very tired (well he *assumed* he was feeling tired, but for all he knew it could be a simple case of ambrosia deprivation, seeing as he had missed breakfast yet again), Gabriel paused outside room 86 and forced despair into the deepest recesses of his angelic consciousness. Ignoring the unabated verbal barrage in his left ear, the punk in the parka opened the door of the room and walked in.

"Come on then, Gabriel, what exactly *are* we going to do? Can't you see it's all over? We're finished! *He's* here! *He's* on this side of the divide and *He's* going to eat us, spit us out and eat us again!"

Sitting round the coffee table in the small but comfortable hotel room, with the full-sized head of Marcus Enderholt resting on the mahogany surface, Embram and Gabriel returned to their true forms. Fifi Lamoure, in her three headed guise, investigated the contents of the mini-bar. As the torrent of verbal panic from the cherub's head increased, Gabriel rubbed his temples and thought of home.

"No one told me that *He* would be involved in any of this! I thought you said *He* was also missing, you thick lizard. And getting *Him* back was *your* part of the mission, you useless scaled worm!"

OK, this would be a good point in the story to have another reflective interlude, and debate not only the stress level of a pissed-off gargoyle, on a scale of 1 to 10, but also the pros and cons of fast food. Well, my friends, if a mark of 1 equates to no stress at all, and a score of 10 represents lots and lots of stress, the particular gargoyle we are all familiar with would score 100. And as for fast food ...

It happened so suddenly that even Gabriel was taken by surprise. (Not a common occurrence for an Archangel of his elevated position, but taking into account the pressure he'd been under since arriving, he felt a surprise or two was acceptable under the circumstances.) Quickly reaching out a clawed hand, Embram Ferret Frightener scooped up the head, growled deeply and tossed it behind him, where Cerberus opened the mouth of the middle head and swallowed it whole. As the absence of sound permeated the hotel room, neither of them spoke as they sat savouring the unexpected peace. It was Gabriel who broke the silence, trying in vain to stop the smile that now spread across his face.

"Oops! Looks like you've done it this time, Embram!"

Looking across the table at each other, they both collapsed in fits of uncontrollable laughter. For a full five minutes the gargoyle and the Archangel lost all self-control; the two immortal creatures crushing their wings as they rolled about helplessly on the carpeted floor. As her six bloodshot eyes took in the unusual scene, Fifi 'Cerberus' Lamoure's middle head belched loudly. Then, licking all three pairs of lips, she settled down to sleep off the unexpected meal. Finally sitting up cross-legged on the floor, Gabriel straightened his wings and waited for calm to return before speaking again.

"Well! That's one for the book, I suppose. Who would have guessed Enderholt would meet such an un-dignified end ... and such a messy one at that?"

Stretching his tattered wings, Embram Ferret Frightener re-positioned his tail, sat down opposite the angel and tried to hide the obvious amusement which still showed in his voice.

"I'm sorry about that; I don't know what came over me."

"Yes you do, Embram, it was something called a loss of patience, and if *you* hadn't done something, I would have. In any case, what's done is done, so there's no point in crying over spilt cherubim, is there? The only *real* problem *I* have, personally, is just how I'm going to explain to 'you know who' that he is now a cherub short of a full set."

Nodding his sympathy for the Archangel's latest predicament, Embram stared at the carpeted floor for a moment; the furrow in his brow-ridges a clear sign that the gargoyle was deep in thought. Scratching one of his horns, he looked at Gabriel and spoke as firmly as he could, considering the circumstances.

"Two things Gabe ... sorry, I mean Gabriel."

"*Two* things Embram? What are you babbling on about *two* things?"

"There are two things I want to say at this particular time."

Letting his head fall back, Gabriel looked up at the ceiling and felt envious of the mortals on this side of the great divide. They at least could go to sleep. He didn't have such a luxury.

"Sorry, it's three."

The Archangel looked back at the gargoyle. "OK, I'll ask: three what?"

"There are three things I want to say, not two ... well actually it's four things."

"Embram!"

"Yes?"

"Will you just get on with it? You're starting to sound like Cardinal Numero Umero of the Spanish Inquisition and his infamous two question interrogation technique!"

"What? I'm lost ... Cardinal who, and what interrogation technique?"

"He would always select the ugliest people he could find and then ask them just two questions before condemning them to be burned at the stake. Firstly, he would ask if they believed that *God* had made man in *His* image. Of course, to this they would dutifully answer 'yes,' seeing that the scriptures said it was so; and after all the scriptures were the word of *God* written down, were they not? Then he would ask his unfortunate victim that if this was indeed the case, which of course it must be, how come the person was so ugly and therefore could not be in *God's* image after all. A hypothesis that brought about the unarguable conclusion that since *God* could not be ugly, then anyone who is must logically be a witch."

"Are you serious? Now I have to be impressed with that, but are you sure he was one of yours? We had a High Priest of Babel arrive at my collection point a while ago; he also had a way with words ..."

"Yes, Embram, I'm sure he did, but this is getting us absolutely nowhere, so shall we get back to the matter in hand?"

"Which was?"

"The two, three or four god-forsaken things you had to say to me, you annoying little toad!"

Registering 4.5 on the Richter scale, Gabriel's angry voice shattered the light bulbs, broke every bottle in the mini-bar and woke the sleeping three-headed dog. Suddenly plunged into darkness, they sat in silence as the angel's temper slowly subsided. Eventually, in a calmer tone, Gabriel said, "Let there be light!"

The room was illuminated by a new set of bulbs.

"Impressive, Gabe, I must say! That was very impressive indeed."

"The name is Gabriel, remember? And yes, it is impressive. It's a little trick *He* taught me, but it's even more impressive when you combine it with the creation of life. But again that has nothing to do with the original matter in hand, does it Embram? Just say what you were going to say, will you!"

Altering his position on the floor slightly as Cerberus Lamoure moved to lie next to him, Embram Ferret Frightener relaxed a little.

"Just because the number the cherub called happened to belong to the Dark One, it doesn't mean that the Dark One is *actually* on this side of the divide. Unfortunately, I can no more sense the proximity of my boss than you can yours. Their auras are so powerful they nullify themselves to everyone and everything. But if your *He* is here, which we know he should be, then mine will be as far away from here as possible ... if you can understand all of that."

"OK, agreed Embram. And your next point is?"

"I think I can guess what part you want me to play in your new plan, and the answer to the question you have in mind is yes, I will take your place and approach your *Him* ... if that's what it takes to end this bloody mission and clear up the mess."

Archangel Gabriel leaned back against one of the chairs and studied the demon, his angelic eyes searching for any signs of treachery in the gargoyle's face. For a time, before time, he had battled against such creatures in the everlasting war between good and evil, slaying more of them than even *his* limitless memory could recall. But this one was different: this one didn't belong. And that was another first.

Thinking 'Havana', Gabriel placed one of the two cigars that materialised in his mouth, thought 'light' and handed the other to Embram. As they both sat savouring the taste, Gabriel blew a smoke angel and continued his study of the gargoyle.

158

"You know what will happen once my *He* realises what you are, Embram?"

"Of course! I just hope it will be quick and painless, that's all."

Inhaling the rich Cuban cigar smoke deeply, the Archangel looked at the sleeping canine, then back at Embram.

"Tell me, Embram, why are you so ready to sacrifice your very existence for the enemy? I would have thought that all of this would present you with an ideal opportunity to chalk one up for your side. Here we are, you and I, on a joint mission to return the status quo, when something goes terribly wrong and I find myself unable to continue due to the parasitic spell. So why don't you just take advantage of this unforeseen situation and inform your superiors that the door to ultimate power is now wide open?"

"You wouldn't understand if I told you." Blowing a series of interlocking smoke rings, Embram Ferret Frightener stroked the sleeping dog and sighed. "So there is no real point in me explaining, is there?"

"Try me, gargoyle. If I can put up with the never-ending ramblings of Enderholt, I'm sure I can listen to what a friend has to say."

Embram sat open mouthed, the cigar dropping into his lap as Gabriel's last words forced their way into his confused thought processes. For a few moments he was transfixed, his mind attempting to make sense of what his ears had heard. It was the smell of burning gargoyle that broke the spell.

"What the ..." Looking down, Embram's eyes widened as he saw the plume of smoke rising from his middle regions. With a grunt of surprise and growing fear, he started to beat frantically at the small fire that now burned brightly in his lap.

"Oh no! I'm on fire! Fire! Fire! Help me! I'm on fire!"

Still beating at the flames that were now slowly

creeping up his body, Embram Ferret Frightener scrambled to his feet and started to dance around the room, an excited Fifi trying in vain to understand her master's predicament as she ran after him. Gabriel, watching this impromptu yet impressive rendition of the fire-dance (which he had actually seen performed only once before, by the *Hopi and Cheyenne Reservation Surreal Art Group* when they had been on a cultural exchange trip to Tibet), smiled in bewildered amusement at the gargoyle's growing panic.

"Calm down, Embram! It's only fire; something I would have thought would be the last thing that would bother you!"

"Oh no! Oh no! I'm on fire! Please put it out! Put it out! Put it out!"

Thinking 'extinguish', Gabriel watched as Embram's panic subsided with the fire, the dancing gargoyle finally ending his impromptu impression of Gene Kelly as the last flame died out. (For those of you below the age of 55 who have no idea just what a 'Gene Kelly' is, let alone why a gargoyle should want to do an impression of one, I think I had better explain. Gene Kelly was, firstly, a *he*—but not *the He*—and secondly, a famous dancer who performed on film at a time when your grandparents were a lot younger than they are now. If you are over 55 yourself, you are in the age bracket that would allow you to remember him. Anyway ... ah, what's the point, it's getting complicated: so on with the story.) Finally sitting back down opposite Gabriel and cradling the agitated Fifi, Embram's embarrassment was evident by his reddening face.

"Have you something to tell me, Embram?"

It's not easy calming down an over-excited hell-hound; especially when in an agitated state its natural instinct is to use all three tongues to lick anything in reach clean, ready for eating. Trying to ignore Fifi gnawing on his talons, Embram finally spoke, his eyes darting in every direction but at the Archangel. "Arsonphobia."

"What is?"

"The thing I have to tell you."

Thinking 'Cuban cigars' again, Gabriel held the two lit Havanas, pondered on the situation and then decided that maybe it wasn't the best plan of action after all. Cancelling the thought, and the cigars, and thinking 'coffee' instead, he handed Embram one of the two cups of best Bolivian that suddenly materialised on the floor between them. He picked up the other for himself.

"You suffer from Arsonphobia?"

"Yes! So? What of it? It's a common enough fear on this side of the divide, isn't it?" Taking a drink from the steaming cup, Embram grimaced when he realised it was decaffeinated, and thought 'more sugar' to try and hide the taste.

"Yes, Embram, as you say that might be the case here on this side, but you are not from this side, are you? You are a foul demon spawn who has spent the whole of his miserable existence living and working in the fiery pit! You are a minion of Hell, who is employed in a place where the only thing a bad soul will know for an eternity is torment in the flames of everlasting pain! So, my little gargoyle, how is it *you* are terrified of fire?"

"That's the real bummer, Gabriel; I don't know why! Why do you think I'm just a minor gargoyle in charge of an arrival point and not assigned to some other more important job? All I do is count them *in*, and then I have to count them *again*! Where can they run to after I have counted them? Nowhere, that's where! But still they have to be counted again, and again, and again! You have no idea what it is to be a nothing, Gabriel! You could not comprehend what it's like to be in the wrong place at the wrong time ... for an eternity!"

Finishing his coffee the Archangel dismissed the cups, stood up, stretched his wings and sat back down.

"And you think that carrying out my aborted part in the mission will give you that one chance to finally become someone? Is that the reason you decided to do it, Embram? Even though you know what must happen to you after?"

Stroking the middle head of the now sleeping dog, Embram Ferret Frightener shrugged his broad shoulders and nodded. What Gabriel said next unexpectedly increased his level of attention. "Do you know that *His* son was originally to be named Frederick?"

Looking at Gabriel, a picture of puzzlement growing on his scaled face, Embram scratched a horn and shook his head. "Whose son are you talking about?"

"*His* son! Whose son do you think I was talking about? When I was ordered to inform Mary that she was ... well, you know, with child so to speak, the notification sheet stated that the child was to be known as Fred. Can you see my predicament, Embram? Frederick, Son of God, just doesn't cut it, does it? So I changed the name on the form."

Embram sat staring at the angel with wide eyes, a smile slowly forming on his crooked lips as he listened to the story. When Gabriel had finished, the gargoyle let the smile turn into a wide grin. "You did what, Gabriel? You actually changed the name of *His* son? What did *your He* say, and what did *He* do when *He* found out?"

"*He* said nothing. You see, by the time the news reached him, it was too late. This side of the divide was not as full then as it is now, so, by the time a certain winged cherub arrived with the information, there was little that *could* be done. The world as it was then already knew him as Jesus, and that's how it had to stay. But the cherub couldn't leave it there, could he? Oh no! He had to bend *His* ear and convince him that I

162

needed to be taught a lesson. The fat little creep said I had over-stepped my authority, so I was temporarily demoted to the post of *Spiritual Mediator* and spent centuries as *His* spokesperson here in the mortal realm."

Nodding knowingly, the gargoyle suddenly looked at the canine and then back to where Gabriel was sitting. "Winged cherub? Do you mean?"

Pointing at the sleeping dog's ample stomach, Embram's eyes glazed over for a moment as his mind processed the information it was being fed. Then, as a light bulb of understanding lit up inside his head, the gargoyle's grin grew even broader. "So that's why you and Enderholt have a personality clash! He was that cherub, wasn't he?"

"You have it in one, Embram, and I have waited since then for a chance to get even. Now, thanks to you and your three-headed waste disposal system, that time has finally arrived. I owe you one, Embram, and where I come from that is an honour not bestowed lightly by any Archangel. So what will it be? Name your favour."

Regarding the sleeping dog, Embram sighed and thought for a while, his two missing talons re-growing as he gently stroked the blue fur. Looking back at Gabriel, the gargoyle finally answered. "Just two *small* things, if that's allowed."

"Two? Well, that's a little unorthodox, but what's an extra favour between friends? Go on then, what are they?"

"When ..." Embram paused for a few seconds, closing his eyes as if collecting his thoughts before continuing. "When *it* happens ... you know, when *your He* makes yours truly an extinct gargoyle ... I want you to look after Fifi for me and make sure that Mr. Muscles doesn't get her back. You know how fussy his wife Megara is when it comes to housework, and she would blow a fuse every time Fifi caught a lost soul and brought it home. And besides, she hates kebabs: they give her terrible wind!"

"Kebabs give Megara wind?"

"No Gabriel! They give Fifi wind! Please take this seriously; it's my existence we're talking about here, and what happens to my nearest and dearest after it's all over!"

Not really sure what he had actually said wrong, Gabriel just nodded in agreement, and pondered on the rest of infinity looking after a three-headed blue-rinse poodle. He wondered whether or not he should tell Embram that he also loved kebabs. Deciding that ignorance would benefit Embram at this point in the proceedings, the angel replied, "OK, I agree. So what's the second favour?"

Gently lifting the three heads from his lap and placing them on the carpeted floor, Embram stood up and opened his tattered wings.

"I ... I want to find out if I do frighten ferrets."

Forcing back the laugh that threatened to erupt from within, Gabriel stared in amazement at the gargoyle. "You want to *what?*"

"Here I am, having spent all of my existence with the given surname of Ferret Frightener, and I have absolutely no idea what a ferret is, let alone why I should frighten one. So now, as my own personal Armageddon draws near, I would like to finally find out."

Standing up again, Gabriel looked around the hotel room and shook his head slightly. "It's ironic, isn't it? Here I am, the Archangel Gabriel, demon slayer extraordinaire, destroyer of all that is evil, sworn enemy of every denizen of the underworld, and second in grace only to *Him;* in a hotel room on the mortal side of the divide with a demon gargoyle who is about to sacrifice itself for *me* and *my kind.* Do you know what all of this means, Embram? It means that things will never be *quite* the same again. This is possibly the beginning of

164

a new phase in the structure of what is seen as good and evil. A possible ceasefire in what was destined to be an everlasting war. What do you think about that, my friend? Can you comprehend the paradox your sacrifice is going to cause?"

Nodding his horned head knowingly, Embram rubbed his chin with the talons of one hand and sighed deeply before answering. "What does ironic mean?"

Without saying another word, the Archangel thought 'ferret', sat down in the nearest chair and watched as the small furry creature appeared and walked over to where the gargoyle was standing. As the digital clock on the wall registered 7pm, Gabriel realised that it was going to be another long night.

CHAPTER TWENTY TWO

It had been a very long day, as far as days on the mortal side of the divide went. The particular day in question was the second Saturday of the month, the day set aside for the monthly meeting of *The James Tiberius Kirk Appreciation Society*. An after-hours get-together of the dedicated and the downright weird, and an ideal opportunity, for some, to ensure extra sales of the now famous *U(p) S(tairs)* imports. (Also, coincidently, the shop's sixth month of retail trading; even though it was actually only the second as far as mortal time went. This is the benefit of divine status: it is an unarguable fact that if you invent time, then it is yours to manipulate whenever and wherever the whim takes you.)

By the time they had finally cleared the shop of the twenty or so uniformed *Star Trek* groupies (who were, as far as a certain Spock look-alike was concerned, a prime example of what three million years of in-breeding can do in such a small world) the *Next Generation* watch on the wrist of Samuel Nevis read 11.58pm. Outside the thick covering of snow was growing as the storm continued unabated.

"Now it *is* Sunday tomorrow, isn't it Gerald?" Still smarting from having his disappearing Saturday reinstated, Samuel switched off the lights and joined his partner by the front door. "Let's have no mistake about this shall we, Gerald, tomorrow *is* my rest day, isn't it?"

Gerald opened the door and thought 'thaw' as they stepped out into the cold night; the falling snow suddenly arching over and away from them as they made their way to the car park at the rear of the building. It wasn't until they had climbed into the vehicle that he answered. "Theoretically, Lucifer, Sunday is *my* day of rest, if you want to be precise: but after a day like today I think we *both* deserve one."

Pulling out into the snow-covered street, the blue Sierra picked up speed and made its way along deserted roads, the snow melting away exactly 2.3 metres in front of the vehicle as they threaded their way past dozens of abandoned cars. Deciding that another trip in the company of Pink Floyd and their *Dark Side of the Moon* would test even his limited appreciation of 70's music, Samuel quickly thought 'Triumph Bonneville', and smiled as his film era Spock uniform was replaced by a black leather jacket, tight denim jeans and 1950's retro footwear. Ignoring the predictable sigh from the driving seat, James 'Satan' Dean turned the rear-view mirror in his direction, brushed his fingers through his now greasy black hair and admired the words *'LOVE'* and *'HATE'* tattooed across four fingers of each hand.

"Nice hair, Samuel; shame about the shoes though." Gerald stole a glance at the leather-clad biker sitting next to him, his eyes momentarily coming to rest on a pristine pair of blue suede winkle-picker boots. "Are your feet really that pointed?"

Styling his hair into a fair representation of a circa 1958 Elvis Presley, Lucifer thought 'Rock Around the Clock', and began singing along with Bill Haley and the Comets, who had appeared, complete with instruments, on the back seat of the Ford. (Once again remember the Tardis, folks!)

"Very good, Samuel, but do we really need to have them here in person?" Shouting above the noise of the six-piece rock and roll band, Gerald pulled in to an empty car park, thanked the group for the entertainment and sighed as peace once again returned to the interior of the vehicle. Switching off the engine and lights, he paused for a moment before speaking again, his omni-mind seemingly momentarily elsewhere.

"Samuel? If there was something I'm not seeing, you would tell me, wouldn't you?"

"Something you're not seeing?" Lucifer Presley thought 'cigarette', and inhaled deeply as he slid down in the seat, resting his booted feet on the dashboard as he stared out into the darkness. "As far as I can see everything is as we want it to be, Gerald; no divine responsibilities, no minions crawling about trying to gain our favour, and no internal audits! Everything is just raspberry, my old mate, just raspberry."

"Peachy, Samuel, I believe the saying you are attempting to master is 'everything is just peachy'. A raspberry is quite a different kettle of fish, and one of my better fruit creations, even if I do say so myself."

"Hang on, Gerald, if a raspberry is a fruit, why then is it with a load of fish in a kettle? That doesn't make sense, even to me."

"It's a metaphor, Samuel: a grammatical statement where a comparison is made between two seemingly unrelated subjects. Typically, a first object is described as being a second object. In this way, the first object can be economically described because implicit and explicit attributes from the second object can be used to fill in the description of the first ..."

"Yeah! Yeah! OK, whatever. But what *exactly* is it you are asking? Is there something wrong, Gerald?"

Materialising a plastic ashtray on to his friend's lap, Gerald listened to the ticking of the slowly cooling engine as snow started to cover the car once again.

"There's nothing wrong as such. I'm just having difficulty sensing anything or anyone from either of our realms. I know we both have a myriad of agents here; I should do, I assigned mine myself, but ever since arriving I've had no sensation of their presence. I'm getting no spiritual response at all! It's as if you and I are here alone, Samuel: alone without any contact from home. Let's just say it unnerves me, I'm so used to being so, you know, omni; that's all it is."

Exhaling the acrid cigarette smoke into the shape of a naked succubus and then sucking it back into his mouth again, Samuel contemplated his non-existent navel and rested a hand gently on his colleague's knee.

"I wouldn't let it worry you, Gerald. I've been having the same problem since we arrived, so I understand exactly what you mean. I'm guessing it's one of those annoying cross-over traits we've been hearing about lately, but I must admit it was so much easier in the past. Take, for example, the time I visited a certain young Maid of Orléans and convinced her it was *you* she was talking to. Now *that* was some barbeque, if my memory serves me right: roasted martyr, bagels and mulled wine, all free for the taking. You have to admit, Gerald, they certainly knew how to throw a party in those days."

Shaking his head, Gerald let the Kirk face fall away as they climbed out of the car. Leaning on the roof of the vehicle, he looked up into the night sky and shrugged his shoulders as the steadily falling snow started to cover them both.

"I suppose you're right, Samuel. The last time I paid a visit to this side of the divide was as a burning bush, and a great deal seems to have changed since then. I seem to be a little out of touch, and for an omni being that's about as non-omni as you can get."

"You've been busy, Gerald; we've both been busy. But we are here on this side for a well earned holiday for a millennium or two, and we *are* going to enjoy it. Just forget about the divine bit and leave the committee to do all the hard work. When we return you can reap all the benefits, like I intend to."

Walking round the car and past his friend, Samuel, whose black leather jacket was now adorned with a painting of his true form, surrounded by the words 'The Real Hell's Angel', walked up to the door of the building that contained their flat, thought 'open' and entered. As he disappeared from view, his voice echoed round the car park. "Don't let it worry you, Gerald; things are going to be just as they should be ... soon, very soon."

Following his friend through the door and down the luxuriously carpeted inner hallway, Gerald re-adjusted his face as he stopped outside the open door of the apartment, his thoughts running through the conversation he and Nevis had just had.

Should he be worried, he asked himself? Maybe he should phone home and check that everything was as he had left it. Or maybe he should just accept that even *he* was susceptible to at least a mild form of 'cross-over syndrome' on this side of the divide. After all, even Lucifer had admitted to his own shortcomings since arriving, and he had been a visitor here on and off since the beginning. Shrugging his omni shoulders and wishing he had spent more time visiting here rather than delegating others to do it for him, Gerald pushed his concerns to the back of his mind and entered the flat.

"Damn this bloody sand! Couldn't you have rented a place from a deity with a little more taste and breeding?"

Lucifer Spock was standing in the middle of the large room, an expanse reminiscent of an ancient burial chamber. The gold-coloured walls were covered with a multitude of paintings depicting various Egyptian gods and goddesses, while hieroglyphics covered an equally gold-coloured ceiling. Papyrus scrolls lay in open boxes on the shelves that lined the walls. Carved stone statues of cats surrounded a large sarcophagus-shaped table in the middle of the room. Oil lamps burned all around, their smoke mixing with that of everlasting incense burners, filling the room with a sweet, sickly smell. Shutting the door behind him, Gerald walked through to the kitchen area and sat down at the wicker breakfast bar. (Its worktop was made from the very best reeds from the banks of the river Ant in Norfolk ... Come on—you didn't really expect reeds from the banks of the Nile did you? Do you know how much it costs to import reeds from Egypt these days?) His hand reached for the cup of Bolivian coffee that appeared in front of him.

"Osiris and Isis owed me one after I turned a blind eye to the husband-brother-sister-wife part of their relationship; and seeing as their place was empty, I decided to call in the favour. In any case, it was a better option than the one you suggested. Can you imagine us living with Baphomet? Not only do goats smell, they also have no decorum when it comes to cleanliness. No, Samuel, I would rather put up with sand in my sandwiches than goat-hair in my bed." Drinking the coffee, Gerald waited for a response from the other room. When none came, he thought 'Bolivian' and smiled to himself as the cup refilled.

In the next room the lights dimmed as Samuel sat down at the sarcophagus-shaped table, his eyes momentarily glowing red as he clasped his hands in front of him. As his teeth grew, so did his smile.

CHAPTER TWENTY THREE

"You look a little disappointed, Embram. I thought the result would have made your miserable day, so to speak." Gabriel adjusted the lay of his wings in the chair as he looked at the gargoyle sitting on the floor opposite him, the creature's downcast eyes an obvious sign of his confused thought processes. "Surely now you know the truth you can change your name to something akin to 'Embram Ferrets' Friend'. Yes, of course you can! So come on, let's see that smile fight its way over that ugly face of yours."

Looking up from his place on the floor, Embram stretched his tattered wings and forced a grin, his crooked fangs showing as he nodded at the Archangel. "I know, Gabriel, and you're right of course! It's just a little bit of an anti-climax, that's all. My father was a 'Ferret Frightener', as was his before him, and the one before that, and so on. So, in a sense, I have just ended the 'Ferret Frightener' hereditary lines, haven't I?"

Gabriel shook his head in amusement and stood up to stretch his wings. "Embram, you are a foul demon spawn from Hell, and like all unnatural creatures you have no hereditary line to end. Your father was just another gargoyle assigned to your nest, as was your mother, your grandfather and all the other gargoyles you have ever known. You didn't have the experience of actually being born, did you? Like me and all the other angels, cherubim, heavenly host and demonic forces, you were created, brought into existence to serve and praise some deity or other. That's our lot, Embram! It's what we all do. It's what we *have* always and *will* always exist for."

Looking down at the small furry creature asleep in his lap, Embram smiled and let a small sigh escape from his lips. He gently picked the ferret up and held it at eye-level. "So you think 'Embram Ferret Friend' sounds good then?"

Contemplating the question himself, the gargoyle stroked the warm fur with one talon, sighed again, and ate the sleeping animal. "No! It doesn't have that ring to it, does it? I think I'll just stick to 'Ferret Frightener' after all!"

Looking up at the ceiling, Gabriel rubbed his temples and contemplated the possibility of returning to the council, admitting defeat and throwing his lot in with them; a possibility which, although contrary to everything he had ever stood for, looked more and more appealing the further the mission collapsed into chaos. Returning his gaze to the gargoyle, he was distracted as the three-headed hell-hound lying next to its master suddenly jumped up, changed back to its alter ego, and looked confused as it said, "Right, that's it! Enough is enough, Gabriel, you conceited lump of Pegasus crap! If you don't sort out this mess I'm going to make your very *existence* unbearable, if and when we ever get back! I've just about had it with you and your pathetic little pet lizard! Do you hear me? I've had it with the both of you!"

Falling backwards in surprise, the Archangel ignored the sudden flurry of feathers as his wings bent against the back of the chair and glared at the dog. At the same instant Embram jumped up, turned to face the canine and stared in open-mouthed disbelief.

"Fifi? You can talk?"

Embram (retaining the family name of Ferret Frightener, thanks in no small part to the involuntary sac-

173

rifice of a stoat named Granville, whose unfortunate fate was to be summoned by an Archangel who, like Embram, had no real idea what a ferret looked like) shook his head slowly as he rubbed both horns. "Did you say *pet lizard*? What do you mean *pet lizard*? After everything we have been through together, is *that* what you think I am: a *pet lizard*?"

Still reeling from the dog's harsh words, the gargoyle snorted steam from both nostrils (which still hurt, no matter which side of the divide he happened to be on) and reached down to pick up the blue-rinse poodle. A firm hand on his arm stopped him and pulled him upright.

"Hang on! Not so fast, Embram, something isn't right here. Since when would this creature bite the hand it feeds on occasionally? It may be a dumb, three-headed flea bitten mutt, but it's *your* mutt. Cerberus may be the foulest, most ill-tempered, nastiest guard dog that ever walked the underworld, but as far as the dog itself is concerned, it's your number one fan ... in fact your *only* fan, I suspect."

Now thoroughly confused, Embram looked from the dog to the Archangel and back to the dog again, groaning audibly before sitting back down on the floor with a resounding thud. "Oh, this is just too much for me to take in all in one go! Are you telling me this *isn't* my Fifi?"

"No, you stupid creature, that's not what I'm saying! I'm saying this isn't *your* bloody *dog* talking!"

"So it's *not* my Fifi then?"

"Yes, it is your damned Fifi! What I'm trying to say is that it's not her bloody talking!"

Gabriel's voice thundered and reverberated around the confines of the small room, the carpet on the floor beginning to dissolve and the paper peeling off the walls under the onslaught of his temper and frustration. As patience pulled its hat over its ears and ran away to hide in some small corner of the Archangel's mind, Gabriel suddenly forced his way past Embram, pushing him to one side in his obvious haste. Kneeling down facing the dog, his mouth next to one of the creature's ears, Gabriel whispered in a low and menacing voice. "I know it's you! I know you're still in there somewhere, you little shit! You can't keep that mouth of yours shut, can you? Well now you're on your own, so let's see you get out of this, shall we? And let's see who has the *last* laugh!"

Moving away from the dog, Gabriel sank into his chair and watched with satisfaction as a wide-eyed Fifi trotted over to where Embram still sat transfixed. Sitting in front of her master, the blue-rinse poodle waited open mouthed as the voice started its tirade of abuse again.

"You do something, lizard! It's your bloody dog, so it's your bloody responsibility! Just get me out of here! Now! Do you hear me? Get me out of here now!"

Recognition came like the dawning of a new day on the mortal side of the divide (that is, of course, just artistic licence again, I'm afraid. In fact, it was more akin to a volcano erupting inside his head, as understanding kicked its way to the forefront of his mind).

"Wait a minute! It's you, isn't it? It's you talking, not my Fifi!"

Tilting his head to one side, Embram snorted steam again and winced at the pain, his brow furrows knotting as anger replaced confusion. Reaching down and picking up the dog, he held it at eye level with one hand and forced open its jaws with the other. Looking directly into the mouth, Embram growled deeply, apologised to Fifi, then spoke in a low, threatening voice. "Get out of my Fifi! Get out of her right now, or you will be *really* sorry. I'm warning you, head, get out of her now *or else!*"

"Or else what, turnip head? You're a worthless, third

rate demon! Just what exactly are you going to do if I don't get out of this putrid pet of yours? And while we're on the subject, just how do you expect me *to* get out? Thanks to your feathered friend I'm just a head, remember."

Steam burst from the gargoyle's nose and ears as his temper erupted, the already peeling wallpaper falling away in sheets as hot vapour filled the small room. As the light bulbs exploded for the second time that night, darkness replaced light and Embram stiffened as he felt the dog being lifted away from his outstretched hands. As the escaping steam ceased, light returned in the form of a glowing Archangel; a radiant figure holding a blue-rinse poodle at arm's length.

"Enough is enough, Embram, this is getting completely out of hand."

Shielding his eyes from the glare, the gargoyle allowed his anger to subside before reaching out for the dog, only to feel it rise again as Gabriel pulled away.

"No, Embram, the head stays inside the dog, do you understand?"

"No I don't understand! I want that thing out of her and I want it out now!"

Placing the bewildered Fifi on the floor between them, the Archangel walked over to Embram, placed a glowing arm around the gargoyle's shoulders and stared at the damp walls. "My dear Embram, there are three *very* good reasons why the head should remain where it is for the foreseeable future. Firstly, while it's in there it can't interfere in what has to be done. And secondly, the more Enderholt suffers, the happier *I* am."

"OK, I can understand those, but what's the third?"

Squeezing Embram's shoulder more tightly, Gabriel grinned, thought 'return' and nodded knowingly as the room reverted to its normal state of repair.

"The *third* reason, my dear Embram? The third

reason is that *I* say so, and that, I believe, is reason enough, is it not?"

As the glow faded, Gabriel returned to his chair and motioned Embram to re-take his place opposite him; a thinly veiled command and one the gargoyle thought it better to comply with under the circumstances. Settling back on to the floor and calling a still confused Fifi to his side, Embram waited while Gabriel found a comfortable position for his wings.

"Eventful night if nothing else, I suppose, but we still have a major problem that is in need of a major solution, do we not, Embram?"

Holding shut the jaws of the dog, who now lay asleep in his lap, Embram Ferret Frightener (or, more correctly, *Embram Stoat Eater*) tried to ignore the muffled voice that was still audible from within and resigned himself to the inevitable conclusion of the conversation. Watching Gabriel as the Archangel conjured up another Havana cigar, Embram tightened his grip on the poodle's jaw.

"Firstly, as we agreed, a soul; and secondly, you're to look after Fifi when it's all over. That's the deal as far as I'm concerned, Gabriel. So will you uphold your end of the bargain if I go through with my part?"

Savouring the rich taste of the hand-rolled cigar he was holding, the Archangel blew a series of interlocking smoke rings and pondered on the real meaning of life (which *isn't* in fact 42 as was previously thought, but *is* connected to the reproduction cycle of a small marsupial living in the space between time and no time. It is an ethereal creature, and one with an imminent extinction problem, due, in no small part, to the unfortunate fact that it's the only one in existence. Confused? So am I, and I'm the one writing this).

"Very well, Embram, you *do* have a deal, but there is one small point which you seem to be overlooking in your calculations."

"That *I'm* overlooking?"

"Yes, Embram, that *you're* overlooking! It concerns a certain boss of yours, and the small task you were sent here to carry out!"

The gargoyle stared into empty space, his mind seemingly concentrating on the wall behind the Arch-angel's chair. Finally he spoke. "Ah, yes, I see what you're saying. But as I said before, if your *He* is here, then mine will be as far away as possible. There is no way in either realm that my *He* would be in the same dimension as yours, let alone in the same mortal place. So let's sort out the current dilemma and let someone else deal with the problem of the missing Dark Lord, shall we?"

Leaning forward, Gabriel re-adjusted his wings and stared intensely at Embram, then down at the dog asleep in his lap. "Come on, Embram, just tell me the real reason you are willing to do this for me. I have always known everything there is to know until now, but you agreeing to sacrifice your very existence in this way has me totally and utterly at a loss!"

Gabriel watched as the gargoyle gently lifted the dog and placed it on the floor before standing up and walking over to the window. Looking out into a snow-laden, early dawn sky, Embram stretched his tattered wings and closed his eyes. "Do you ever remember a time before you were an angel, Gabriel?"

Distracted for a brief moment by the outpourings that had resumed from the sleeping dog's mouth, Gabriel contemplated reaching in and dragging the head out physically; but dismissed the idea after considering the reaction such an act would encourage from the gargoyle. Looking back to where Embram was standing, he shrugged his shoulders.

"No, of course I don't. I came into existence the moment *He* decided to exist himself. So, as there was nothing before him, there was obviously nothing before me. It's a simple concept really, even for you to comprehend. *He* came first, and then I did."

Leaning back in the chair, Gabriel smoked the last of the cigar and wondered if it was really worth asking the inevitable question. Curiosity popped in and said 'go for it,' so he did. "An interesting question, Embram, especially from a creature of your lowly status. Is there a particular reason for asking it, or is this just conversation?"

Turning away from the window, Embram once again took on the appearance of the skater boy, complete with board and hooded sweat top that read, 'Shit's Happening and I've No Toilet Paper'. He popped a well festered spot and walked back over to where Fifi Lamoure still lay sleeping. Sitting on the floor next to her, his skateboard resting on his outstretched legs, skater Embram looked down at his camouflage pattern *Spicoli* boardshorts and sighed. "You wouldn't understand if I told you. How could you? You're the divine Gabriel, Archangel on High and all the rest of that celestial stuff! *Everything* is possible for you, and *everything* is under *your* control!"

"Yeah! Yeah! Embram, I've heard all this before, and every time it's the same!" Looking up at the angel, Embram was sure he saw him deflate slightly, his body sinking slowly into the chair as he looked towards the ceiling and continued: "You think *I* wouldn't understand? You think *I* have no problems? Gargoyle, you have absolutely no idea, do you? You are clueless, Embram! Haven't you understood anything since we arrived here? No, obviously you haven't. You still have no conception what it's like to be me, do you?"

With sudden swiftness, the angel swept the spotty youth up from the floor, pinning him into one of the other chairs. Gabriel's face was almost touching his as the Archangel looked into the teenager's eyes.

"Can you imagine an eternity of having to be right

all of the time? Or the pressure of being the only entity in all of Heaven that *He* completely relies on? No, of course you can't! How could you? You are just another minor cog in the vast and infinite wheel of inter-realm politics! An insignificant pawn in a never-ending game of one-upmanship between two immortal super-powers. So, Embram Ferret Frightener, just what exactly is it you have on your mind that troubles you so much?"

Gabriel returned to his original place in his chair as suddenly as he had left it, leaving a stunned skater boy staring down at the sleeping dog. Trying to gather his thoughts, Embram only looked up when he heard a calmer Gabriel speak again. "So what is it, Embram? What is it that makes you ask such a strange and un-expected question?"

The answer, when it came, brought a look of surprise and bewilderment to the angel's face.

"I dream."

"You do *what?*"

"I dream. I always have, ever since my nesting time."

"But that's not possible! Only mortals, dogs and angels dream."

Looking at the sleeping Fifi at his feet, Embram raised an eyebrow and smiled slightly as the poodle turned over on to her back.

"Does that mean Fifi dreams as well?"

"No Embram, it doesn't! The flea-bitten animal is one of your lot, isn't she? So it stands to reason that she can't dream either! But it's not her we're talking about, is it? *You* can't dream, it's just *not* possible!"

As early morning light started to flood the room through the frozen glass of the window, Embram shrugged and popped another spot.

"Possible or not, I still dream, and it's always the same one over and over again."

"Go on then, tell me about this so-called dream of yours." Blinking twice and ignoring the sudden rattle from his multiple facial piercings, punk Gabriel polished his Union Jack *Doc Martens* on the leg of his suit trousers, materialised another already-lit cigar and settled back in the chair. "And then, just maybe, we'll get on with the more important issue of the modified mission!"

"I dream I'm dead."

"You dream you are dead, do you?" Taking a long draw of cigar smoke, Gabriel contemplated making the dream come true, but decided that humouring the gargoyle was probably a better option for the moment. "I see, but there is one small problem with a dream like that, isn't there Embram?"

"I can't die?"

"That's exactly it, my scaly friend! As we both know, you don't have the option of death; only extinction, and believe me that is far more painful. And nothing comes after it, except for nothing! So all you are really experiencing is wishful thinking, Embram, nothing more and nothing less!"

As we have already discovered, the I.Q. of a gargoyle is nothing to write home about, let alone measure on a scale of 1 to 50. But even under such stressful conditions as those found on the mission, this gargoyle knew when to shut up.

"I suppose you're right, as usual; and in any case, when I meet your *Him*, all of this will end up a pointless exercise for me anyway. Death or extinction isn't much of a choice at the best of times, I suspect. Either way, being vapourised is being vapourised, no matter how you look at it."

Looking away from the youth, Gabriel stared out at the steadily falling snow for a few minutes, the glass of the window thawing as the central heating automatically adjusted itself to the gradually warming air of the room. They sat in silence for a while, lost in their own personal thoughts.

Gabriel finally spoke. "You really are quite an enigma, aren't you Embram?"

"No, I'm not an enigma, I'm a gargoyle!"

Choosing to ignore the remark, Gabriel continued. "In my capacity as the bearer of *His* secret messages to the chosen ones …"

"What secret messages?" Embram looked at Gabriel with renewed interest as the angel continued his inspection of the window.

"If I told you they wouldn't be secret any more, would they Embram?"

"OK, so who are the chosen ones then?"

"They are just 'the chosen ones', Embram, so will you stop asking so many questions and let me do something I am very good at: bathe in my own righteousness and glory? Right, as I was saying before I was interrupted, in my capacity as the bearer of *His* secret messages to the chosen ones, I am often seen as the Archangel of annunciation, humanity, resurrection, heavenly mercy, vengeance, death, revelation, truth and hope. But the most important factor is that I carry *His* word wherever I go, and in spreading *His* word to all who will listen, I am, in fact, a good example of a …"

"A good example of a second-hand car salesman, created with the *brains* of a dead toad and the *morals* of an excommunicated heretic."

As a new stream of insults began to pour from the sleeping dog's mouth, Embram scooped Fifi from the floor and held her close to him, waiting for some new form of retribution to come from the direction of the Archangel. He only relaxed when Gabriel continued talking as if nothing had happened.

"Of an apprentice deity in the making, so to speak. But I digress somewhat; and before you ask, digress has nothing to do with my digestion … if I had one, of course, which I don't." Skater Embram pretended to understand, and grunted in agreement as Gabriel continued without pausing for breath. (Which, as we already know, he has no need to do, seeing as he *is* a heavenly being without equal, and has no need to breathe ... etc. etc. etc.) "What I'm trying to say is that in all my eternity of existence, I have never actually met a creature quite like yourself. You look like a demon, you definitely smell like a demon and you even shuffle about like a demon."

"I do not shuffle!"

"Believe me, Embram, you shuffle. I've met and destroyed enough demons to know you *all* shuffle, whether it's on two legs or twenty-two. You *all* walk as if you've eaten a bad curry the night before! So trust me on this one Embram: you shuffle, OK? Right, where was I? Ah yes, as I was saying, in all of my wonderful existence I have never met one quite like you, my horned friend: you simply do not fit the well formulated criteria for your standard, everyday demon. You are just not ..."

Looking back to where the gargoyle-in-human-form was sitting, Gabriel paused for a moment as he straightened his multi-coloured Mohican, his head tilting slightly as he contemplated the best term to use. "You are just not of evil demon stock, are you Embram?"

Looking down at the dog yawning in his lap, Embram the skater boy stroked the blue fur and let a resigned look settle on his spotty face. Brushing the greasy hair out of his eyes, he smiled slightly and nodded.

"You have it in a sea-shell, dude."

"I think you mean I have it in a nut-shell. The saying is 'nut-shell', Embram."

"A nut-shell? Wow, you mean like chestnuts roasting on an open fire? And Jingle Bells you merry gentlemen? Oh, I love Christmas! Hanging my socks up and stuffing the vulture, and all that white snow spray in a can ..." Positive that his ears had suddenly been stuffed full of wet ectoplasm (a substance that in fact *does* exist, but unlike what most mediums believe is nothing more than spiritual ear wax), Gabriel shook his head and stopped Embram in mid-sentence.

"Wait a minute! What do *you* know about Christmas?"

"I know Satan Claws always forgets me and that it's impossible to get a tree that doesn't catch fire as soon as I get it home. But besides that, not much I'm afraid. I'm sure I could get hold of a book on the subject if you're interested."

OK, here is a small test of your memory and its ability to recall specific information. Do you remember, early in the book, reading about a *lack* of patience attributed to this particular Archangel? You do? Good. So if something terrible and heinous were to happen at this point, and a certain gargoyle-in-human-form was to be violently torn into very small pieces and fed to his own dog, you wouldn't be at all surprised?

Well let's see shall we?

Deciding that the falling snow outside was a preferable sight at the moment, Gabriel looked back at the window and thought of home, forcing back an overwhelming urge to bring forth the ten plagues of Egypt upon the small room and one of its occupants. He took a deep breath (which he didn't really have to) and looked back at the young teenager, who was still stroking the fur of the now wide-awake poodle.

"I really don't want to know any more details, Embram. It's obvious that you're nothing like any of the usual run-of-the-mill demons, and because of this you just don't fit anywhere, do you? I'm guessing that's been your problem since the beginning. But that's all irrelevant now. All that matters is that you do what is necessary, so that the status quo can be restored."

"Restored? They're not that old, are they?"

"What? Who?"

"Status Quo, of course!"

Gabriel sighed loudly. Taking the hint, Embram returned to the original subject of their conversation. "And the deal, dude? Is the deal still on?"

"The deal is sealed, Embram. I will ensure that the dog is cared for, and it will stay with me until the end of known, and unknown, time."

"And what about the soul thing, Gabe? Will I still get one of those after it's all over?"

Again choosing to ignore the disrespect the angel smiled before answering. "Ah yes, that soul business! Well, there may be a small problem with that part of the bargain, I'm afraid. You see, *He* will eliminate you and erase any memory of your existence. And even if you already had a soul it would make no difference in the long run. Divine extermination is *total*, with no provision for an afterlife or even a long-lived memory. Even the dog will forget you ever existed, and as far as I, myself, am concerned, you will have been just an irritating nightmare. Sorry!"

For the first time since having to stop Queen Vashti from stripping down to her birthday-suit in front of the court of King Ahasuerus of Persia in 460BC, Gabriel felt genuinely sorry for his actions. Watching as Fifi lifted her head and licked at the youth's spotty face, Gabriel asked the question he knew he had to have an answer to. "Does that make a difference to your decision, Embram?"

Smiling as the dog continued to wash his face, the skater gargoyle changed the words on his hooded top to read, 'The Afterlife Is A Bitch ... But She's My Bitch', sniffed, and placed the animal back on to the floor.

"Yeah, dude, I'll go through with it. In any case, Fate told me that at some point in my existence something would happen that I wouldn't like, so what's the use in postponing the inevitable, as they say."

"You know one of the Fates?"

"Yeah, dude, Koltho attends the same group therapy sessions as I do. It was her who said I would meet a tall, handsome stranger one day, but I suppose she can't be right *all* of the time." Standing up and walking over to the mini-bar, Embram picked up one of the miniature bottles of vodka, opened it and drank the contents. "So when do we get this over with, Gabe? I guess the sooner the better as far as I'm concerned, so shall we go now?"

"No, today is the Sabbath: *His* day of rest, so we wait until tomorrow. In the meantime, is there anything you wish to do, or maybe experience before ... you know, the end?"

Thinking for a moment, Embram Ferret Frightener picked his nose and examined the fluorescent green slime clinging to his finger before wiping it on the leg of his shorts and turning to face the punk angel.

"OK, if they're good enough for *Him* then they're good enough for me, so bring them on, Gabe, my main man, and lets kick start this three creature party!"

Wishing he *didn't* have to, Gabriel resigned himself to asking yet another question he knew could only bring him discomfort. "Exactly *who* is it you want me to 'bring on,' Embram?"

"Black Sabbath of course! Oh, and yes, there is *one* more *small* thing I would like you to do for me when we eventually leave here and head out for my grand finale ..."

It was going to be a long Sunday, thought Gabriel. A very long Sunday.

PART THREE

'THE VOYAGE HOME
(IF WE'RE LUCKY)'

CHAPTER TWENTY FOUR

"If I were mortal, I think I would hate Mondays just as much as mortals do! In fact, I believe I would hate them even more, seeing as it was me who decided Monday should come directly after Sunday, which *is* part of the weekend after all."

Lucifer Spock, feeling slightly out of place dressed as he was in full Vulcan ceremonial robes and sporting longer hair than usual (a film era uniform was one thing, but Vulcan robes and long hair?), glared at Gerald as the Kirk look-alike unlocked the door of the shop and continued the one-sided conversation.

"The Sabbath day just seems to fly by, doesn't it? No sooner have we had Sunday dinner, it seems, than the alarm is going off on Monday morning. The week just drags until the weekend arrives, then the time seems to disappear. It's just very ..."

"Gerald! Will you *please* shut up? I'm beginning to think that living amongst these pathetic little creatures is starting to rub off on you! Maybe coming here wasn't such a good idea after all. Perhaps we should have opened a 'Soul Cleaning Agency' in Purgatory instead. At least there I wouldn't have any sinuses to get sinusitis in, would I?" Samuel Nevis pinched the bridge of his pointed nose with the thumb and fore-finger of his left hand and silently cursed his own, personal nasal cross-over affliction. "But we're here and business is blooming, so I suppose a perpetual pain in the nose is a small price to pay!"

"Booming, Samuel, business is booming not 'blooming'." Gerald pushed open the door of the shop, switched on the lights and walked over to the alarm panel. Lucifer Spock followed. "In any case, Samuel, the 'Soul Cleaning' franchise in Purgatory is exploited enough, so I hear, and if my memory serves me right, which of course it *always* does, didn't you put in an official complaint about that a while back?"

Handing James T. God one of the two mugs of coffee that had suddenly appeared on the counter, Lucifer Spock watched as his friend adjusted the display stands, preparing the shop for the line of customers that was already starting to form outside.

"OK! OK! So I made a complaint or two about that, but what did you expect? All I was trying to do was to make a living, that's all, and what do these 'soul laundrettes' do? I'll tell you what they do, shall I? They wash away sin and polish a tarnished soul brighter than an Archangel's halo! Now that's what I call unfair, don't you? Do you know how many souls I've lost because of Purgatory's free trade policy? Have you any idea how many of the damned have been cleaned and reprieved in these establishments?"

"Actually I do, Samuel. Seeing as I *am* God, I know everything there is to know about everything. At the last count, which was just after the UK release of *The Search for Spock* I believe, the total stood at ..."

"OK! You've made your point, Gerald! There's no need to expand on it, so let's just open the shop and let in these pathetic creatures, shall we?"

Shrugging, Gerald adjusted the alignment of his Kirk face and turned the 'closed' sign on the door to 'open'. As the first wave of customers entered the shop, Samuel growled deeply and made his way to the stairs. Reaching them and looking back into the now crowded shop, he said, "I'll go and check on the latest delivery of 'U.S. Imports' shall I?" Not waiting for an answer, he turned and climbed the stairs. As he did, the growl deepened.

Nodding politely, the smartly dressed woman at the reception desk watched with obvious distaste as the spotty youth clad in boarding shorts and hooded top emblazoned with the words 'The End Is Nigh ... But My End Is Bigger', carrying a skateboard under one arm and a blue-rinse poodle under the other, approached.

"Can I *help* you, sir?" The tone of her voice reflected the growing revulsion she was feeling as she looked down her long nose at the teenager.

"The cool dude and I," the youth said, motioning with a nod of the head towards the punk rocker standing by the revolving door, "will be leaving your establishment now, and will not be returning I'm afraid ... well, at least, *I* won't be returning, but I can't speak for my main man. Maybe someday *he* will return, well that is, of course, if I'm successful. But I digress somewhat! You see, *I* have a task to perform, a task on which *your* very existence, and the existence of every other mortal, depends. So, before I leave and carry out my kamikaze mission ... what are the chances of a kiss?"

Embram skater boy caught the stapler in mid-flight, the skateboard falling to the floor with a resounding clatter as he reacted to her obvious rejection of his request. As the young woman's face reddened with anger, Embram pulled a baseball hat from his back pocket, placed it obliquely on to his head and jumped onto the board.

"Ah well, your loss babe! She has no idea just what she is missing, does she Fifi?" Planting a wet kiss directly on to the lips of the dog, skater boy winked at the woman, spun the board round 180 degrees and set off in the direction of the angel and the revolving door. As the youth sped away from the desk, the colour suddenly drained from the receptionist's face; not because of the obnoxious boy looking for a cheap thrill, but because, as a parting shot, his dog said, "Believe me, you didn't want his lips anywhere near yours, or near any other part of your pathetic body!"

"You just can't leave it alone, can you? You always have to humiliate yourself, and anyone else who happens to be around you! It happens every time!" For the few people brave enough to venture out into the continuing snowstorm this particular Monday morning, the sight that greeted them would be one they would remember for a very long time. Standing on the path outside the hotel, one hand holding Fifi at eye-level, the other prising her jaws open, the punk Gabriel was looking into the dog's mouth and talking, to all intents and purposes, down the animal's throat.

"Well that is *it,* Enderholt!" (Marcus Enderholt the Third he still was, at the moment, but almost certain to be Marcus Enderholt the last if Gabriel had his way.) "As far as *I'm* concerned, you tapeworm, you can live in there with the rest of the garbage, and that fat, little headless body of yours can wander for an eternity looking for the rest of you!"

Watching from a safe distance (just what *is* a safe distance from an irate and pissed-off Archangel, I hear you asking? Well, I have no idea, but you can bet it's a very, very long way), skater Embram fought back an overwhelming urge to grab the dog and run. Instead, he gritted his teeth and waited for the Archangel's anger to subside.

"You get me out of here right now, Gabriel! Get me out, or else!"

Forcing the jaws even wider, the Archangel brought the open mouth closer to his face and peered into the dark cavern. The thought of the head's predicament brought a feeling of satisfaction he hadn't experienced for a very long time. (In fact, not since he managed to persuade the arrogant Archangel Raphael that just

192

because he was the angel of science and knowledge, it *didn't* give him the ethical right to clone himself.)

"Or else what? No, Enderholt, this time you've cooked up once too often!"

"He's *cocked* up, Gabriel."

Looking over at the skater boy, the punk Archangel frowned. "What did you say?"

"I said he's *cocked* up, Gabriel. I think that the terminology you *should* be using is that the Enderholt head has *cocked up*, and not 'cooked up'."

Glaring at the youth for a moment, Gabriel shook his head and returned his attention to the dog's mouth.

"Like I said, Enderholt, this time you've *cocked up* once too often." He cast a sarcastic smile Embram's way and continued. "I will ensure that you never see the light of day ever again ... except through one small opening, if you get my meaning!"

Dropping the dog back onto the ground, Gabriel sighed and stared at the snow-covered street in front of them, his multi-coloured hair becoming whiter with every passing moment as he became more and more lost in thought. Finally, thinking 'parka' and pulling up the fur-lined hood, he turned to Embram (now clad in his own parka, with an obviously disgruntled Fifi sitting unsteadily in the hood) and forced a smile.

"Well, this is it, I suppose, Embram. No point in prolonging the inevitable longer than we have to. So the sooner you carry out your part of the bargain, the sooner I can ..." Looking at the dog settling itself deeper into the hood of the gargoyle's coat, Gabriel let the smile turn into a grin. "... the sooner *we* can go home."

Walking past the youth and his still-mumbling dog, Gabriel headed up the street towards the northern side of the city, the falling snow now parting as it flowed round him like water around the keel of a ship.

"There is just *one* small problem, dude!" Embram called after him.

"And that is?"

"Just a *minor* point really, my main man, and one I'm a little hesitant to mention considering the pressure you've been under, but ..."

Gabriel stopped and turned. "But what, Embram? What are you trying to say?"

"But we have no idea where your *He* is, do we?"

Pulling back the hood, punk Gabriel looked up to the grey, snow-laden sky and smiled again before walking on. "Actually I do. I just forgot to mention it."

CHAPTER TWENTY FIVE

Instinct told him where he was heading. He knew, without thinking, his ultimate destination and only one purpose filled his primitive consciousness now: only one last task to perform and it would finally be over for him. Then all would be complete ... and oblivion would reign (or snow, considering the weather lately).

Walking steadily through the wind-driven snow, he forced his way through small groups of people rushing from shop to shop, ignoring their complaints, heading out towards the northern suburbs of the city. As he turned into the almost deserted shopping arcade, he stopped suddenly and looked down.

"Are you Father Christmas, mister? Are you? Are you?"

The voice came from a small girl, bundled up in a thick coat, long scarf and yellow fur-lined boots, standing on her own directly in front of him.

"Are you? Are you Father Christmas and have you got a present for me? Have you? Have you? Please say you have, and can I have it now? Please? Pleeease can I have it *now*?"

Bending down, his long white hair falling over his face, he examined the small figure intently as his canine teeth began to grow, his eyes slowly darkening into pools of blackness. Reaching in to the top of his red leathers, he grinned broadly as the small child looked on wide-eyed with anticipation. Bringing his hand back into view, he licked his lips and handed over a small parcel wrapped in Christmas paper and finished off with a pink ribbon tied neatly in a bow.

"Yes! Yes!" the girl squealed. "I thought it was you, I really, really did! What is it in the box? Is it a kitten? No, it's too small for that! Is it a PlayStation game? No, it's too big for that! I know, it's an MP3 player, isn't it? Yes, that's what it is, I know it is!"

As the girl tore at the wrapping paper, her eyes never leaving her new found treasure, he let his own eyes return to normal and resumed his dedicated journey. As he reached the corner, half way along the arcade, he heard a small voice echo behind him, "Hey! Wait a minute. My name's *not* Pandora!"

His grin grew as he heard the lid of the box open ...

The two skateboards wove their way along the streets, past abandoned cars and deserted shops, through traffic lights that directed no traffic, onwards towards the place they had to be.

"If this *ever* gets back home I will *never* live it down!" His multi-coloured hair once again white with snow, punk Gabriel spoke in a guarded growl in the direction of the youth riding next to him, the wheels of the boards melting the snow as they continued on their way.

"I hope you can hear me, Enderholt! *One* word, *one* small word about any of this and you will rot in there for the rest of eternity, or even longer!"

As Fifi settled herself deeper into the hood of his parka, Embram looked at the skateboarding angel and winked.

"Wow! I'm impressed, dude, really impressed! Who would have ever guessed an Archangel could board! Hey! Do you sky-board as well? You know, with the wings and all."

Narrowly missing a woman wrestling with a pram in the deepening snow, Gabriel regained his balance and shook his head. "Yes, I've sky-boarded before, and I should have guessed this would be that extra thing you wanted from me! My *He* went through a 'modernisation' phase a couple of millennia or so ago and decided that sky-boards were going to be the great replacement for the 'Chariots of Heavenly Fire'. But, as with a lot of *His* radical ideas, it never really caught on with the more conservative amongst us."

"Wow!" the teenager shouted back, as he successfully negotiated his way between two pensioners struggling to keep upright in the snow, their Zimmer-frames sliding from one side of the path to the other. "And I bet a certain Eric Von Daniken didn't like that idea either! I can see the book cover now, can't you, Gabe, my main babe? Von Daniken's controversial publication of 'Skateboards Of Fire' subtitled, 'Was God a Boarder?' "

Shouting a belated apology to the pensioners as he followed the youth, and knocking away both Zimmer-frames in the process, skater punk Gabriel caught up and glared at Embram.

"I am not *your* or anyone else's 'BABE'! The title of 'dude' I will put up with! I will even tolerate 'my main man' if I must. But under no circumstances will I answer to 'BABE'!"

Increasing their speed, they lapsed into silence for a while as they approached the north end of the city, each preparing himself for whatever was to come. Finally, overtaking the adolescent, Gabriel brought his board to a halt and stared across the deserted road. Embram narrowly avoided colliding with him.

"*He's* in there!" Pointing through the falling snow to one of the shops opposite them, the angel spoke almost in a whisper. "And I'm assuming that this is as far as I can go with any margin of safety, so from this point on, Embram, you're on your own."

Dismissing both boards with a simple thought and

lifting Fifi from her place in the hood of his parka, Embram's gaze followed the direction of Gabriel's outstretched finger and he inwardly shrank as he realised that the time had finally arrived. Picking up the dog, he sighed, nodded, and started to cross the road. Gabriel's hand on his shoulder and a strange shiver down his back brought his head around.

"Just a little trick that may come in handy, Embram. You never know, you may want to call this Scotty fellow and 'beam out of there' at some point."

Confused by who this Scotty might be and what the Archangel meant by needing to 'beam out', Embram shrugged and continued across the deserted road.

As the snowstorm began to increase in severity, Gabriel squatted beside the wall and waited...

The shop was as full, as it usually was by 10am; the till constantly opening and closing, the shelves gradually emptying of the day's stock. The Kirk and Spock look-alikes drank their continuous supply of coffee and watched with satisfaction.

"We will be able to retire soon at this rate, Samuel. Another few months of this and the world will be our oyster, so to speak." They were standing behind the counter, arms folded, watching the continuing stream of customers. "In fact, we *could* retire now if we wanted to, and never work another day in our lives," Gerald Oliver Davis continued.

Placing his 'Better The Devil You Know' coffee mug on the counter and watching as it refilled itself, Samuel Allen Trevor Anthony Nevis straightened his Vulcan robes and head-band and looked at his captain.

"Gerald, I hate to burst your celestial bubble, but the world *is* your oyster! And just to clear up another point, how *can* we retire, seeing as we are already retired? In any case, where in all the known and unknown cosmos would you like to retire *to?*"

198

Gerald considered for a moment as he served a pale-faced Data clone (or Lore, I suppose; but that depends, of course, on whether or not you ever watched any episodes of *The Next Generation*). The pimply youth was so eager about his purchase of the whole of the fifth season of *Deep Space Nine* on DVD that he tried to exit the shop through the closed door, without actually trying to open it first.

"Weston-Super-Mare!"

Lucifer Spock stopped casting a minor irritation spell on a nearby customer and looked at his colleague.

"What about Weston-Super-Mare?"

"That's the place I would like to retire to. That is, of course, as you point out, *if* I was intending to retire in the general sense of the word."

"Are you being serious, Gerald? Isn't that the place you dumped all the rubbish you had left over after the creation of the universe?"

Smiling at a young woman bearing a striking resemblance to the terminator in *Terminator 3*, Gerald handed over the signed copy of Stephen King's *Salem's Lot* she had just purchased and watched as she walked out of the shop. Placing the money in the till, the James T. Kirk look-alike waited for the next customer to approach the counter before carrying on with the conversation.

"No, that was Manchester! Weston-Super-Mare is the place Moses chose to practise the parting of the Red Sea. Practised, and practised, and practised, if my sources are to be believed."

Nodding knowingly, Lucifer Spock quickly hexed a nearby teenager's acne and carried on serving. "That explains the mud. Stirring up the seabed over and over again must have caused ecological havoc, not to mention the financial damage to the fishing industry in the area."

Positive that his omni-senses must have failed him for a moment, Gerald ignored what he *knew* he couldn't really have heard and waited for some sarcastic remark to follow the out-of-character statement. When none came, he carried on with the business of making a profit. As his friend left the main shop to bring down new stock from the upstairs room, the Buddhist prayer bell above the shop door heralded the arrival of yet another new customer.

The youth in combat shorts, hooded top, Nike trainers and green parka shook the snow from his baseball cap and looked around the crowded shop, his eyes pausing momentarily on each of the customers as he made his way carefully towards the counter, a blue-rinse poodle close at his heels. The spotty teenager suddenly stopped, his face becoming ashen as his gaze fell upon Captain James T. Kirk, now only feet away from where he stood. Through his demon's eyes he saw an altogether different sight from anyone else, and one that brought with it an impossible wetness that crept from the front of his shorts to the back. As his non-existent bowels also decided that the time was at hand for a movement, Embram Ferret Frightener scooped up the dog, turned and headed back the way he had come. A sing-song voice from deep within the animal reached his ears before he was half way to the door.

"You leave now, lizard, and it's all over!" Although the voice came as no real surprise to him, the words stopped Embram in mid-stride. "But then again, what more should I have expected from such a *pathetic creature* as you! Gabriel is a fool to think you would actually go through with this! You may have fooled him, but you're not fooling me, Eberzam, or *whatever* you're called! Once a demon, always a demon! An unarguable fact that you are now proving to be correct!

So why don't you just run away and hide until it's all over? Go on, run!"

In his confused and terrified mind he knew that running away was the only option he had. Ahead of him stood the door and on the other side of that door an Archangel: one who would turn his decapitated head into a candle-holder, and send it to live with the cherub's inside his precious Fifi. But it was what happened next that helped force any thought of flight from the gargoyle. As panic filled most of his mind, a new sound emerged from the open mouth of the canine; the sound of a chicken in full cluck, quickly followed by a new barrage of abuse. Every pair of eyes in the room was suddenly directed towards him.

"Chicken! Chick! Chick! Chick! Chick! *Chicken!"*

Holding the dog at arm's length, he glared furiously into its open mouth, steam starting to escape from his nostrils.

"Look everyone, it's Embram Chicken Kisser!" the voice continued, unabating. "Or is it Embram Chicken Licker? Or *maybe* it's just Embram the *CHICKEN!"*

Fighting hard to keep up the illusion of his human disguise, Embram felt any self-control he may have once possessed start to run away, as his rage grew in intensity. He was approaching breaking point when a firm hand on his shoulder brought him spinning round: "Is there anything the staff at *The Captain's Log* can get for you, son?"

Looking down at feet encased in open-toed, brown leather sandals, Embram's eyes carried on up the white robed torso and past a badge that said 'Just Ignore Me, I'm Going Through A Mid-Millennium Crisis'. They paused at the head, which sported a flowing, white beard and was topped by long, white hair. As each spot on his greasy face exploded involuntarily, skater Embram dropped the dog and stood staring at the figure standing in front of him.

"Ah! No! I mean yes! I think I mean ... Oh mother! Please do it without me looking, so the agony is over quickly!"

To the others watching, Captain James T. Kirk stood staring at the youth for a few moments as the shop returned to normal. To Embram, the old man in flowing robes was preparing to obliterate his very existence. He knew the time had arrived when the old man reached out and took hold of his arm.

"You look ill, son. I think maybe you had better sit down for a while. Would you like a coffee, or a glass of water?"

Unable to control the fear imp that was now filling him with other members of its family, like terror and panic, Embram Ferret Frightener allowed himself to be led, like a lamb to the slaughter, to a nearby chair. Sitting down, he watched in a semi-dazed state as Fifi joined him, then looked up at the architect of all his fears, who was still standing right beside him.

"Right! That's better, isn't it? You just sit there until you feel better, and then feel free to look around. If you should need any help or advice, please do not hesitate to ask."

Now, as I'm sure you have already noticed, the ability of a gargoyle's mind to define the nature of what *is* and what *should be* is rather limited, to say the least. This was the problem that a certain gargoyle we all know and love was struggling with at that very instant.

Scratching his head through the mop of greasy hair, skater boy stared in confusion as the unprotected old man walked amongst the throng of strangely-dressed mortals, seemingly ignoring the fact that not a metre away sat a demon gargoyle, fresh from the foul pits of Hell (well OK, maybe not *fresh*, but he didn't smell *that* bad). Somewhere in the confusion that was his mind, a tiny voice cried out that things were far from how they should be. He should be gone by now, his existence scattered to the far reaches of whatever there was beyond his understanding. But instead here he was, sitting within a claw's reach of his ultimate enemy, and still existing. Standing up and lifting the seemingly unconcerned poodle, Embram clamped the dog's mouth shut with one hand, and spoke.

"Ah, excuse me! I said excuse me, sir!" As he spoke, he felt a shiver run down his spine as his non-existent bladder contemplated the possibility of evacuation once more. "I know what you have to do, so if you will just let me have my say, you can carry on and do it."

Turning round to face him, the old man smiled, shrugged his robed shoulders and reached out to stroke the dog. "That's OK, son, I can re-fill the shelves later, there's no real urgency to do it now. So, what is it I can get for you? DVDs, an autographed poster maybe, or how about an 'I'm A Ferrengi, And I'm All Ears' sweat shirt? I even think we have dog sizes in stock."

"No! No! I don't want a bloody sweat shirt! Tell me something, will you? Is this some form of 'tease the gargoyle before you rip him apart' joke? If it *is*, then I'm *not* laughing! Do you hear me? *I'm not laughing!*"

Transferring his hand from Fifi to Embram's arm, the robed man smiled sympathetically and offered him a steaming cup of coffee.

"That's fine, son, just fine. Tell you what, why not forget the sweat shirt and sit yourself back down and have a coffee? In my experience, everything always looks different after a nice mug of Columbian bean."

OK, let's pause here for a moment and consider the situation that Embram finds himself in. Here he is, a demon gargoyle from the dark underworld, standing next to *GOD* himself and still existing! Here is our unsung hero (I know! I know! Maybe *hero* is a little of

203

an overstatement, but let's give him a little credit, shall we?) preparing to sacrifice his very existence for the *other side*, and what's happening? He is being ignored, that's what! Now how ironic is that?

For a very, very, brief moment skater boy Embram Ferret Frightener forgot where he *was* and *who* he was with. Reaching up, he grasped the front of the white robe and pulled the old man downwards until the bearded face was level with his own.

"Listen to me, will you! I may be a nothing to you and your precious kind, but I *demand* that you at least treat me with the respect you would offer any other foul spawn!"

Smiling, the old man nodded and pulled free from the youth. "Now, now, lad! I'm sure your *mother* doesn't think of you as a foul spawn, does she? So why on earth should *I* see you as one, let alone treat you like one?"

"Mother? What in the Nine Rings has my mother got to do with this?" Once again all eyes were turned their way as his voice went up an octave, steam now escaping *up* his nostrils and into the vastness of his almost empty brain cavity. "You are going to listen to me, even if I have to pin you to the ..."

Now, either it was the hot steam that filled his head, or a random thought process that for once didn't just leak away, that brought the sudden glimmer of under-standing. Either way, Embram stopped his outburst mid-sentence and forced himself to re-evaluate the situation. As the room around them returned to normal, Embram dropped the poodle to the floor, growled deeply and snapped his fingers twice. All around them time ceased to exist, the crowd of customers frozen in a pocket of nothingness. Embram bent down and retrieved the dog.

"Wait a minute (a silly statement to make, really,

seeing as a minute has no meaning at this point), how did *you* do that?" The old man looked round the shop, then back at the boy. "Only two of us know how to do that! Two of us and a very select group of our most trusted!"

"I gathered that! And I believe one of your *most* trusted is a certain Archangel named Gabriel, if I'm not mistaken?"

The robed figure stared at Embram, his eyes narrowing as he stroked his white beard. "You're telling me you were taught that little party trick by the Archangel Gabriel?"

"No, that's *not* what I'm saying!" Finding himself backed up against a wall, Embram realised that his sense of direction, walking backwards, was just as bad as it was walking forwards. "What I *am* saying is that I'm here with Gabriel and I have to do what Gabriel *can't* do, but *should* be doing ... if you get my meaning."

"So if you're with Gabriel and you are also here to see me, then you must be one of mine as well!"

If he hadn't been so terrified the whole scenario would have seemed farcical. As he pushed back harder against the wall, Embram squeezed the dog and tried very hard to sound calm. He failed. "Am I one of yours? Ah, well yes, and then again, no. I suppose at this moment I could be technically classified as one of yours, but, then again, I'm not."

As the old man crossed his arms and studied him intently, Embram looked away and concentrated his gaze on one of the frozen-in-time customers. Nervously picking at the poodle's blue fur with his fingers, skater boy felt a new sensation, as something wet started to trickle down his pale face.

"You're sweating, son. Is there something wrong? Or is there something you wish to tell me, maybe?"

Now he knew how all those damned souls felt when

they reached his arrival point, a wave of absolute terror and despair sweeping over him as he stood helplessly facing the old man. Lifting Fifi up to his face and squeezing her one last time, Embram let a smile cross his lips as she licked him, then placed her gently on the floor. Closing his eyes momentarily, he gathered together what little mental strength he had left and prepared for the end. He was about to speak when the door suddenly opened, a flurry of snow entering the confines of the shop and instantly freezing in time, hanging suspended in the air like some bizarre ice sculpture. What appeared in the open doorway not only confused him completely, but also set alarm bells ringing deep within his limited psyche.

Framed in the ice-covered doorway, its long, pure white hair hanging neatly over its narrow shoulders and half way down its back, stood the wraith. Its intense black eyes scanned the room. When its gaze fell upon them the wraith stepped forward and entered the shop. As it crossed the threshold a dark shadow filled the room, bringing with it an oppressive atmosphere that grew in intensity as the shadow darkened.

"So, you have both finally arrived. Good ... so *now* it can begin!"

The voice came from the rear of the shop. The gargoyle's attention was torn away from the white-haired wraith as a long buried memory screamed its way to the forefront of his mind. As recognition dawned his non-existent bladder finally gave up, releasing its non-existent contents down his human leg and on to the floor.

Embram had heard that voice only once before, and that was a very, very, long time ago. He had been in his first age, a period when he had taken up the post of *Apprentice Arrivals Officer* in one of Hell's quieter areas. He had just finished an in-house training course,

206

based on the traditional and well proven style of torment, coming under the heading of 'soul termination, using pointed things and sharp teeth' (a tried and tested formula with a pedigree stretching back to the days of Cain and Abel, that has now fallen from favour due to the new politically correct practice of 'soul distraction, using various mind altering drugs'), when a delegation from *Angel Falls* had arrived for a surprise inspection. The delegation was headed by *the man* himself.

Embram hadn't actually seen *the man*. He hadn't even been in the same building when the delegation discovered a celestial spy masquerading as a cleaning wraith in the *Department of Top Secret Torments*. But half of Hell, including Embram, had *heard* the rage of the Dark One's fury exploding when the breech of security was discovered. (Actually, just to put the record straight, the spy story was just that ... a story. What *really* happened was a simple case of a werewolf tormentor mistaking *the man's* leg for a tree, and relieving itself of a bladder full of stagnant water. Not really a very dignified experience for the one known as 'Foul Lord of All Things Evil'; consequently, the story became something of an urban legend.) It was a sound he would never forget, so when the same voice suddenly filled the shop, he knew he wanted oblivion more than anything else. Forcing his eyes in the direction of the voice, Embram felt his bones turn to jelly as his gaze fell upon the last thing he wanted to see ... ever! At the bottom of the flight of stairs at the back of the shop, dressed in an immaculate blue pinstripe suit, blue silk shirt and matching tie, stood the only permanent resident of *Angel Falls*. The cloven hooves were barely visible beneath the expensive material of the Italian-cut trousers; the horns, polished to perfection, protruded from immaculately styled hair. Unable to stop either the saliva that dribbled from the corner of his skater boy mouth, or the strange smell emanating from his lower regions, Embram (now more scared than any ferret could *ever* be) lost all control of his mouth and babbled like he had never babbled before.

"It's you, isn't it? Yes it's you, I know it is! I was just about to ... no, I wasn't *about to*, I was defiantly *going to* ... Or was I? Is it you? Please say it's not ..."

"There, Gerald, now can you see the problems I've been having? Just look at the quality of staff I have to work with these days: it's no wonder target figures are down on the previous millennium's audit!"

Licking a finger with his forked tongue and running it along the length of both eyebrows, Lucifer (no longer Spock) looked at the old robed man standing in the middle of the shop, his arms still folded as if nothing unusual was happening. Clicking his well manicured fingers once, Lucifer ignored the bright flash that turned skater boy Embram back into gargoyle Embram, and took no notice of the clap of thunder that heralded the gargoyle's instantaneous arrival next to the wraith.

"That's better! both my boys together in one place. Tell you what, why don't you two get acquainted while Gerald and I have a little chat?" As the wraith's head turned towards the terrified Embram, the gargoyle let a very pathetic grin form on his face and babbled something about the wraith's hair and how much it must cost to keep it so white. As his sanity committed suicide, Embram Ferret Frightener called for his mother and wet himself again.

Leaning against the counter, examining the black nail-varnish that adorned the tip of each of his claws, Lucifer smiled condescendingly at his one-time business partner.

"I expect this is a bit of a surprise, isn't it Gerald? One minute we are running a lucrative retail outlet selling all kinds of rubbish to these monkeys and the

208

next I'm dropping a demonic bombshell and cutting short your vacation. I just *love* surprises, especially ones that have a happy ending ... for me that is!"

Standing in the same spot he had occupied since the re-appearance of his colleague Mr. Lucifer from the stock room, his arms still folded across his chest, Gerald Oliver Davies said nothing as Beelzebub in blue continued his speech. (Incidentally, a speech he had been practising on and off ever since the 12th Century, when God himself had officially sanctioned a certain Witchy Hannah Shripmere's honorary position as the president of the *Witches & Warlocks Dyslexia Association, Non-Denominational Branch:* a post Lucifer had promised to his friend and bridge partner Genghis Khan.)

"And just to show how much I've valued our long-term business partnership, Gerald, I have one or two extra surprises up my very expensive sleeve especially for you. I do hope you like surprises, Gerald, because these will make you smile ... or maybe not."

Brushing a speck of dirt from the lapel of his jacket and straightening the knot in his silk tie, the Dark Lord was about to continue when Gerald unfolded his arms, changed the wording on his badge to read 'Same Shit, Different Reality', and finally spoke. "Surprises you say, Samuel? I see. And I don't suppose by any stretch of a mortal's imagination that these surprises will be beneficial to anyone else but yourself? No, of course not! After all, it's the nature of the beast, isn't it? Sorry about the witticism Samuel, but you are, if nothing else, always predictable."

Forcing his eyes down to the unimpressed looking Fifi sitting at his feet, Embram cringed as he heard the last part of Gerald's reply and waited for the inevitable response. His wait was short.

"PREDICTABLE! You think I'm *predictable* do you?" The light dimmed further and a hot wind suddenly blew around the interior of the shop, the shelves and their contents spontaneously combusting as Lucifer's rage exploded around them.

"I'll show you predictability, you pompous, second-rate deity! Let's see how you worm your way out of this one, shall we?"

The indoor storm grew and the air was suddenly filled with the pungent smell of sulphur (thanks in no small part to Embram, whose non-existent bowels had once again surrendered). Embram Ferret Frightener glanced down at the unconcerned Fifi again and tried to ignore the look of open contempt directed at him by the wraith. Closing his eyes tightly, the gargoyle cowered as thunder joined the increasing chorus of noise.

With flames dancing in his hair, Lucifer leaned forward on cloven hooves, glaring at his adversary as he allowed a broad smile to grow slowly on his face.

"It's time for a change, Gerald!" The anger in his voice was gone, replaced by an almost mocking tone. Although no longer shouting, his words could still be heard, even above the cacophony of sound. "You've become far too complacent in your *very old* age, and complacency is an old friend of mine."

Embram was about to wish himself into oblivion when Gerald Oliver Davies clicked his fingers: a small movement that immediately plunged the room into silence, unbroken until he himself spoke again a few seconds later.

"You were about to inform me of the surprises you had in store for me, Samuel, were you not? Well, let me assist you in that area, if I may." Changing the words on his badge to read 'I Don't Give A Fig About Dates', Gerald sneezed and nodded with satisfaction as the showroom returned to normal. "I may be omni, but I didn't need supernatural powers to know about the fake parasite spell you ordered your wraith to cast on Gabriel to keep him out of the way. *Neither* do I have

210

to have second sight to know all about your personal involvement in the committees' plans to amalgamate the two realms. It may also *surprise* you to know that it was *me* who changed the orders concerning the choice of the demon that was to accompany Gabriel."

Pausing, more for effect than anything else, Gerald thought 'Bolivian coffee' and took a drink from the steaming mug that appeared in his hand.

"And as for the quaint 'anti-sensation' spell you have continued to surround me with? Well, Samuel, the *cross-over syndrome* excuse would have been far more convincing if I had been anyone else. But, as usual, you have underestimated my long reach. A reach that extends past anything you could ever imagine, Samuel. You see, I've known from the very beginning that you would try this at some point. I am God after all. But I have never known when, or how. Even a God has his limitations, it seems. So when you suggested that we go A.W.O.L., I decided to incorporate your deceit into my own plan of action. Here in the mortal realm we are on neutral ground. Both of our powers are limited, but I have the distinct advantage of being forewarned, if not forearmed!"

Levitating himself, Lucifer sat down on the counter and nodded slightly as the smile appeared on his lips again. Leaning his head to one side, he let the smile turn into a mocking frown.

"So, Gerald, once again you seem to have me at a disadvantage, do you not? Or have you? Yes, I agree my powers are limited here, but as you so correctly point out, so are yours; so I decided on a plan of action that would compensate for any little hiccups that might crop up. You see, Gerald, we have an interesting and unique situation here, do we not? Here we are, you and I, the two of us living in the mortal plane with limited powers and, let's face it shall we, vulnerable."

Embram edged slightly away from the wraith, who

was now visibly drooling at the mouth as his master spoke.

"*But* Gerald, and it is a big *but* (I know, I know, there's a joke in there somewhere, but come on! This is a dramatic part of the book: the big climax to the story, so let's have a little decorum, shall we?), I seem to find myself at a slight advantage for a change. Here *you* are, alone in a primitive environment, and where is your precious Archangel Gabriel? I'll tell you where the great demon slayer is, shall I? The pathetic creature is out there somewhere, hiding away because he chose to believe rumour and supposition. Of course I must admit that my boy over there ..." Waving a hand in the direction of the wraith, Lucifer continued, "was one of my more ingenious ideas. But unfortunately my second rate scientists couldn't perfect the parasite spell, so I modified my original blueprint to suit the situation."

Letting the mug refill itself, Gerald thought 'chair' and sat down in the leather armchair that appeared behind him. Taking a drink, he changed from his robes into jeans, white trainers and a white hooded sweat-shirt with an embossed picture of William Shatner surrounded by a halo and the words, 'Trekkies Do It Boldly', and a new badge that read, 'Klingons Make A Mess Of Your Shorts'.

"And your point, Lucifer, is?"

"My point, Gerald? My point, as you so simply put it, is that you may be forewarned but I have the vastly more important advantages of superior numbers, excessive firepower and a very unpleasant surprise that you seem to know nothing about!"

Crossing his legs in mid-air and polishing his hooves with the sleeve of his suit jacket, Lucifer leaned forward and winked at the older man.

"Let's examine the power structure as it stands, shall we Gerald? Firstly, we have my own considerable powers: reduced, I admit, but still a force to be reckoned with, as I'm sure you will agree. Secondly, we have the gargoyle. Limited as it is in actual demonic powers, it can still make a nasty mess of even the most resilient spiritual being with its claws and fangs. Then we have its ..."

Looking at Fifi sitting quietly at Embram's feet, Lucifer sniggered, not bothering to hide the look of contempt that appeared on his face. "Its pet, or whatever it is! The only thing I can really say is that three heads are better than one, and three sets of teeth are even better."

Pausing, as if waiting for some reaction from the old man sitting opposite, Lucifer rubbed both hands along his horns. When no reaction came, he carried on with his speech. "And so, Gerald, we come to the grand surprise! The penultimate scene in this tragic play! Now my old friend, I *can* still call you that, can't I? No? Oh well! Now we come to my little secret, Gerald; and surprise, surprise, it's stood just over there!"

Pointing once again at the wraith, Lucifer grinned smugly and produced a glass of sparkling French Champagne which he drank down in one gulp, the flames in his hair turning from red to blue, then back to red again.

"I see, Lucifer. It looks as if you have everything all sewn up after all. But there is just one small thing that's puzzling me." Looking at the wraith with disinterest, Gerald dismissed the refillable coffee mug and rested his head against the back of the leather chair.

"I may be outnumbered, outgunned, or whatever other term you may want to use. I may have even been outwitted this time. But what I can't *quite* understand is just what you hope to gain from all of this, Samuel? You know, as well as I do, that there are a number of important constants in our line of work that can never be changed or altered in *any* way. I've always known it was you behind the instigation of the two committees, and I must admit to a little admiration on my part at the extent of your influence in that particular area. But in the same way my influence is quite wide-ranging as well, so I've known the basics of this plan of yours for some time. So when you suggested that we did our disappearing act, I decided that the time had arrived to find out just what you are up to, my friend. So here we are, on reasonably neutral ground, and I'm biding my time waiting to see what you have up the sleeve of that very expensive suit of yours."

Feeling more than a little nauseous, Embram listened to the verbal exchange between the two supreme beings and once again edged away from the drooling wraith. It was at this point in time (or no time, depending on your perspective! If you happened to be one of the Trekkie customers, you would believe your-self stuck in a 'Temporal Anomaly', no doubt brought on by a worm-hole suddenly appearing somewhere on earth, or at least in its immediate vicinity. On the other hand, if you happened to be Embram Ferret Frightener, you would see the situation in a completely different light ... and still feel sick!) that his collapsing thought processes suddenly remembered something he had heard earlier.

"Wait a moment!" He had spoken even before he realised it.

Quickly turning his gaze back to the floor as a certain pair of black eyes suddenly looked his way, Embram waited for the feeling of terror to worm its way through his body and out of his ears, before allowing himself to think again.

It took a while for the facts to re-emerge from the mush that was now his brain. It took a little longer for his brain to fully understand the meaning of what he had heard. The wraith *hadn't* cast a parasite spell on Gabriel. It had been some form of disorientation hex, deliberately designed to confuse *even* an Archangel.

214

That, combined with the misinformation he and the head had, inadvertently, given the angel had been enough to make the subterfuge complete. Here he was, completely out of his depth, involved in a situation neither he nor Gabriel could ever have foreseen. Things were going from bad to worse and Embram knew only *two* sure things ... It was all over. And he wanted his mother!

CHAPTER TWENTY SIX

The few people braving the falling snow tried to ignore the obviously homeless punk rocker squatting against the wall of the school grounds. Those who found they couldn't dropped a few coins in front of him before rushing on. Ignoring them as if they didn't exist, Gabriel stared intently at the shop opposite and cursed having to send a simpleton like the gargoyle on such an important mission. Resisting the almost overwhelming urge to follow Embram into the shop, the Archangel fought back his frustration and continued to wait for some sign of success. Or failure!

As Gabriel watched and waited, Embram realised there was no chance of informing the angel of the changed situation. He was on his own, and whatever happened from here would happen no matter what he did ... or didn't do.

"So Gerald, you are patiently waiting for my next move are you? Well, it seems that your information is far from complete, old friend, and for an Omni being that *is* a little unusual."

"Yes, it is a little unusual Samuel, but as you very well know, things have been a little hectic over the past millennium or two in *both* our camps. So I can be forgiven if I haven't had my finger on the pulse all of the time, can't I? But no matter what I've *missed* Samuel, I have still kept one step ahead of you throughout all of this!"

Levitating away from the counter, Lucifer slowly let his polished cloven hooves touch the floor and walked over to where the wraith and the petrified Embram still stood. As the wraith frothed at the mouth with excitement, Embram closed his eyes as tightly as he could and tried to ignore the warm wetness running down his leg.

"As you say Gerald, you have been kept very well informed over the past millennium or so, and that intrigues me. It's obvious you have a mole, or some other furry creature, passing you information. But what puzzles me is the importance of the information you have been privy to."

Turning to face the gargoyle, Lucifer looked down at the spreading pool of water on the floor and shook his head. "Well there's one thing for certain, Gerald, *whatever* it is you know it didn't come from this wretched creature! So, am I to know? Or is this going to turn into an inter-realm game of 'Guess the Spy'?"

"Now *that* depends if there's a prize for the winner, doesn't it?" A new voice resounded from the back of the shop as a sudden puff of fluorescent green smoke heralded the arrival of someone, or something, else. As the identity of the new arrival became apparent to those in the room, Embram quickly decided that oblivion was now, without doubt, the best choice. Resigning himself to an eternity of infinite pain, Embram Ferret Frightener waited …

"Simon? This *is* a pleasant surprise, but I do hope there is a very good reason why my managing director isn't in his office and why he isn't finalising the merger personally." Lucifer didn't even turn to face the newcomer. "But knowing you as I do, I'm sure there is."

Walking into the main area of the shop, the small, fat, balding man, dressed in an expensive looking dinner suit, stopped half way between the two deities and inhaled on the small cigar he was carrying.

"I do believe it's Embram Ferret Frightener, is it not?" the man said, looking in the direction of the terrified gargoyle, then at the dog sitting at Embram's feet. "And, of course, Cerberus ... sorry, I mean Fifi. I must say, the blue fur is quite unusual for a dog of your talents, and the guise of a poodle is also a little odd. But then again I prefer cats myself."

Moving his attention to the wraith, Simon Sharp nodded and studied the creature for a brief moment, his face expressionless as he stared at it. "And *that* must be *it*, if I'm not mistaken, Lucifer? I've signed so many budget requisition slips during its creation that I feel I know it almost intimately."

"OK Simon, enough! I'm sure Gerald has no interest in how much we spend on defence. Besides, you still haven't answered my question. Just why are you here?"

Walking over to where Gerald was still sitting in his leather armchair, Simon Sharp nodded to the older man and let a full set of feathered wings grow through the cloth of his jacket. Moving behind the chair and standing with his hands on the old man's shoulders, Simon Sharp smiled as Gerald Oliver Davies broke one of his own commandments (but not the one about 'Thou shalt not covet thy neighbour's Marijuana plants', which, as we already know, wasn't one of his anyway. If Moses had ever found out about Heaven's carefully hidden greenhouse complex he would have had kittens, or whatever other pet was in favour at the time) and took his own name in vain.

"My God, Lucifer! I sometimes wonder if you have any of the sense you were created with! Do you *really* think I would just let you get on and run things your way without even having a backup plan of my own? I'm omni remember? I know *where* you are, *where* you have been and *what* you do! I even know what this creature is!" Waving a hand towards the wraith, God didn't give Lucifer a chance to interrupt as he continued, "I even know what its true function is and what it does! Oh, and by the way, have I introduced you two? Lucifer, meet the Archangel Simon: the first Archangel I created, and, if you remember, the first demon *you think* you created."

The room exploded in a blast of wind, lightning and thunder as the Dark Lord's temper once again erupted. Staggering under the onslaught, Embram reeled as he felt his master's anger and fury burning into him, his eyes snapping open as he braced himself against the arm of the wraith, which stood solid against the hot wind. As the rage subsided and the room returned to as near normality as it could under the circumstances, Embram took stock of arms, legs and other parts of his anatomy, then looked quickly around the shop. Still sitting in the armchair, with Archangel Simon standing directly behind him, Gerald looked totally unconcerned by the display. Bringing another mug of coffee into existence, he took a drink and watched as the flames surrounding his adversary subsided.

"Temper, temper, Lucifer! There's no need to go over the top, is there? It's over, so why not just accept that you've lost this battle as well. Look, shall we all just go home and prepare for the next time? It's been fun in its own way, and I must admit that I've enjoyed my time pretending to be like them ..." He nodded towards the group of frozen Trekkies, "but it's time we both returned to our homes. I have to sort out the mess the committee's made while they were under *your* influence, and you need to seriously re-evaluate your security systems."

Finishing his coffee and dismissing the mug, the old man stood up and was about to depart when the grin that had appeared on the face of the Dark One made him suddenly very, very suspicious ...

It hit him so unexpectedly that he fell forwards into the snow-covered road, rolling him over on to his back so that he found himself staring up into the grey snow-laden sky. It felt as if someone, or something, had just used his own sword on him; a series of painful spasms running in ever constricting circles around his head, finally subsiding into a dull ache. Standing up quickly, Gabriel knew instinctively that such pain could come from one place and one place only. What he had felt was a surge of concern from *Him*—a wave of apprehension that he knew could not be ignored. Reaching for his sword and finding only the brown leather belt that held up his suit trousers, punk Gabriel cursed aloud, forgot about the hex and started to run across the road towards the shop. He had just burst through the door when the fun began ...

Lucifer's grin grew broader as he saw the growing concern on the old man's face, his eyes darkening until they became totally black. Ignoring the whining that came from the direction of the gargoyle, the Fallen One shook his head slowly and spoke in a low growl.

"So you think I'm beaten do you, Gerald? Well, I suggest you think again before you celebrate another notch on your celestial harp! You see, you may *know* what the creature was designed for and you may even know what it is. But there are two things you obviously *don't* seem to know, Gerald. Firstly, the wraith isn't so much a spell carrier, but more of an actual spell. You see, my *old* friend, I have never lived under the delusion that I could ever make you an *extinct* divine being: that particular task is beyond even *my* considerable powers. But, what is the *one* thing I could do that would make a serious dent in that confidence of yours? Give up? Very well, let me enlighten you. The one creation you are proud of above all others is this, the mortal realm. So I designed our friend over there to carry out one task, and one task only ..."

Pausing, more for his own pleasure than anything

else, Lucifer watched in ecstasy as the calm expression on Gerald's face fell away, with understanding replacing complacency.

"Even *you* wouldn't dare to go that far!" Gerald Oliver Davies had invented panic to teach Adam and Eve a lesson when they had gone apple scrumping. Now he wished he hadn't, as panic started to fill him, from his shoes upwards.

"Oh, but I *would*, Gerald! In fact, you can bet your immortal life that I'm *going* to do it! Just call it sweet revenge for eons of being subservient to you. You can wave goodbye to all of this; and there is nothing you can say, or do, that will stop what is about to happen to your precious mortal realm! If I can't have *all* their mortal souls, Gerald, then neither will you! As I'm sure you have already worked out, my boy over there is a walking, talking, all singing and all dancing Doomsday Spell, designed for one purpose and one purpose only. And thanks to my propaganda department, and, of course a certain Mr. J. Goebbels, not even my own side knew the *full* facts behind the project ... and that includes *you* Simon!"

Turning to face the wraith, the old man beckoned to the angel behind his chair and ordered him to deactivate the weapon before it was too late. Looking somewhat perplexed, Archangel Simon smiled and shook his head as an important memory filtered through.

"There's nothing to worry about, nothing at all. I've been involved with this project from the beginning, and although it's been on a purely administrative level, I've gained enough knowledge to understand the basics of its workings. Look at its eyes: the weapon isn't activated or they would be glowing red. Until they do it's just a harmless toy, so just give me the order and I'll destroy it now!"

The look of relief that formed on the old man's face was short-lived, as Lucifer looked at him and said in a clear and condescending voice, "Simon has a good point, to be fair, Gerald, but do you remember I said I had one *last* surprise for you? Well, here's the *real* bummer, Mr. 'Oh, so Divine' Gerald Oliver Davies! You see, there is only *one* thing that can activate my little toy, and that *one* thing is about to make its usual dramatic entrance: round about ... now!"

(For anyone with a nervous disposition: you may want to look away at this point, and practise screaming with your eyes shut in readiness for the film version.)

As the figure burst through the ice-shrouded doorway, Embram Ferret Frightener finally fully understood the plan. It was as simple as it was brilliant: a strategy that even he could appreciate. Lucifer had relied on two important factors to finalise his little scheme. Firstly, even the *thought* of losing the mortal realm would send *any* God worth his weight in angels into a panic. In itself this was an unheard-of occurrence that would send shock waves through the fabric of time and space and onwards into infinity. The event would cause a continuous ripple that would be felt by every celestial being on this side of the divide, including the arrogant Archangel by the name of Gabriel. This brought him to the second and most cunning part of the plan. When Gabriel felt the effects of the ripple, what would that egotistical and single-minded Archangel do? (Answers on a postcard, please!) He would forget everything: that's what he would do. Forget that his close proximity to his God would bring about Armageddon! Forget everything they had talked about! And forget about poor Embram! It was the part of the plan that couldn't fail. Gabriel *would* come! Of that Embram had no doubt ... no doubt at all.

As the punk Archangel made his usual dramatic entrance into the shop, Embram's expression said 'Please bugger off ... NOW!' and the wraith's eyes started to glow red.

Waves of celestial panic swamped him as he entered, the sheer force of the storm within almost knocking him back through the doorway and into the street. Bracing himself, Gabriel quickly looked round the room, then wished he hadn't. Standing by the counter with a look of smug satisfaction on his face was the angel's ultimate enemy. Opposite sat Gabriel's *Him*, his divine face ashen and etched with something Gabriel couldn't believe he was seeing ... fear.

Standing behind the chair, obviously completely out of his depth and babbling like the gargoyle, was another angel; unknown to Gabriel, but at this point also unimportant. His eyes were drawn to the two figures standing in the middle of the room.

The wraith's eyes glowed so brightly that the room was now bathed in red by their brilliance. From its mouth bubbled a stream of froth and steam poured from its ears as it whistled like a demented kettle. Next to it stood Embram, his face contorted in terror as he faced the Archangel, pleading for him to do something. ... Anything.

"It's a bomb thing!" screamed Embram, trying to be heard over the noise of the wraith on it's final countdown. "It's going to explode and take the whole of the mortal realm with it, and probably more!"

As the wraith's eyes started to melt, Gabriel stepped over to Embram and locked eyes with him.

"Two to beam up, Scotty! Come on, Embram, think! Two to beam up!" Reaching down and picking up the dog, Gabriel placed a hand gently on the gargoyle's shoulder and said softly, "The needs of the many outweigh the needs of the one, Embram."

"WHAT?" As confusion joined forces with terror on his face, Embram Ferret Frightener shook his head in disbelief. "What the hell are you talking about, Gabriel?"

Squeezing the scaly shoulder gently, Archangel Gabriel leaned forward and whispered in the gargoyle's ear, "I have been—and always will be—your friend, Embram! Two to beam out, Scotty ..."

Suddenly understanding swept away the terror and confusion as a strange feeling of calm washed over him. Now he understood *why* he was here, realised what Gabriel had imparted to him that moment just before he had crossed the road on his way to the shop. As Embram Ferret Frightener finally realised what he had to do, he smiled his crooked smile at the angel, then looked at the dog. "Look after her, Gabriel, and remember: no kebabs!"

Glancing back at the Archangel, Embram allowed the crooked smile to spread as he turned and wrapped both arms around the boiling wraith. Closing his eyes tightly, he spoke for the very last time: "Energise."

The room returned to normality the moment the two figures disappeared. Time resumed its steady progress and groups of uniformed customers carried on living out their *Star Trek* fantasy as if nothing had happened. Looking around, Gabriel searched for the one he knew he had to confront. He found that Lucifer had gone.

"You didn't expect him to hang about did you, Gabriel?" Turning to face the owner of the voice, the angel bowed his head slightly as he came face to face with the captain of the original *Enterprise*. "He's gone back to lick his wounds and plan his next attempt to get the better of me: something I'm sure will happen sooner rather than later. And talking about later, I suppose I should be grateful this was a case of 'better late than never', Gabriel. Just *don't* cut it so fine next time!"

Allowing a feeling of relief to nudge him, Gabriel looked over the captain's shoulder at the other Archangel (now dressed in an ensign's uniform from the film era and preparing to teleport home) and spoke in a low whisper. "Who's the new boy?"

Walking over to the door and turning the 'open' sign

to 'closed', Gerald waited for the last customer to leave the shop before sitting back down and answering the question.

"That, Gabriel, is a very, very long story, and one that can wait for another time and place. And talking about stories, I believe you have a few things to explain yourself, have you not? A number of points concerning a certain demon gargoyle named Embram Ferret Frightener?"

Nodding, Gabriel changed back into regulation guise and straightened the straps on his armour before thinking 'chair'. Settling into the white, synthetic leather recliner opposite the captain, the Archangel took the cup of Bolivian he was offered, picked up the sleepy Fifi and, placing her on his lap, proceeded to relay his report.

"Well, who would have thought it?" Gerald Oliver Davies sat drinking his hundredth cup of coffee as Gabriel finished his narrative, his Kirk face staring up at the ceiling as he contemplated what he had been told. "It just goes to show that you should never judge a gargoyle by the size of its feet, doesn't it?"

Not even bothering to ask, the angel nodded politely and let his captain continue, an eternity of experience telling him that it just wasn't worth enquiring.

"I've just had a message from internal security. The committee have been detained and are awaiting my return. It seems that a certain demon agent calling itself Julia Hewitt infiltrated their ranks a millennium or so ago. So it looks as if the revolution is over, Gabriel. We can all go back to the Heaven we remember."

Nodding in agreement, Archangel Gabriel was about to comment when the captain leaned forward and said quietly, "One small thing, Gabriel. I believe you have a little something that belongs to me!"

"I do?"

"Yes, I think you do. Well, to be precise, you have part of something that belongs to me."

Stroking the sleeping dog, Gabriel might have wished that the earth could open up and swallow him, but he had no intention of ending up *you-know-where*. Blushing slightly (not an easy task for a being with nothing to blush with), the Archangel forced a nod and shrugged his broad shoulders.

"You mean the head?"

"No, Gabriel, I don't mean just the head! I mean the disconnected portion of Marcus Enderholt the Third (definitely *not* feeling very *Randy* any more, especially after spending time inside a three-headed hell-hound with a digestive problem). His body has been causing major problems at home, wandering around in search of its head!"

Looking at the floor as he thought hard for a way out of the predicament, Archangel Gabriel resigned himself to bearing the brunt of the captain's displeasure. He looked back to where God was sitting, still drinking coffee.

"Point taken, Big G, but you don't suppose I could just ..."

"No, Gabriel, you can't keep it in there a bit longer. I'm one short of a set as it is; and besides, how would you explain away the fact that Cerberus can now talk?"

"Ventriloquism?"

"Nice try, Gabriel, but no! Just remove the cherub's head and I'll ensure that it's reunited with its other half."

Sighing quietly, the angel forced open the mouth of the sleeping dog. As he did, he wished he hadn't. "And about time too, you festering, winged turd! When my union is through with you and that pathetic excuse for an extinct lizard, you are both going to wish the wraith had ..."

The voice was suddenly cut off mid-sentence as a

226

hand, attached to an arm in an original series uniform, clamped the dog's jaws shut.

"Maybe you *should* keep it in there just a little longer. I'm sure we can find a place to store the body if we look hard enough. But Gabriel, no more candles! OK?"

Failing to hide the smile that appeared on his Kirk face, Gerald Oliver Davies stroked the dog, then let a more serious look take over. "There is one more thing before we go home."

Gabriel looked at him and frowned, unsure but thinking hard, trying to recall if there were any other loose ends that he had overlooked.

"Is there? I'm sorry but I don't quite follow."

"The gargoyle. You know what *happened* here, don't you?"

"Yes, Sir, he saved your mortal realm from total annihilation. He teleported himself and the wraith to the space between time and no time, where it self-destructed harmlessly."

"What was your impression of the creature, Gabriel? And be totally straight with me, like you always are!"

Leaning back in the chair, the Archangel looked at Fifi sleeping in his lap and paused before answering. "I liked him. He was an unfortunate example of some-thing being created in the wrong place at the wrong time. Yes, he was a demon on the surface, *nothing* could have been that ugly without being a foul spawn from Hell. But inside, he was about as evil as one of those tormentor bugs Lucifer leaves lying around the place. A nuisance and a pain in the rear at times, yes, but evil? No, Big G, Embram was a lot of annoying things, but deep down inside he was OK."

"Thank you, Gabriel, you've just confirmed what Archangel Simon has already told me. *His* words were a little more colourful than yours, especially concerning the Karaoke evenings and the Elvis impersonations, but on the whole he agreed with you. So, Gabriel, what are we to do?"

"Can I be completely open and off the record, Sir?" Stroking the dog, Gabriel thought hard before continuing.

"I wouldn't have you any other way, Gabriel; and yes, off the record *is* OK."

"When it came to the end, Embram went out the way I hope I do when my time comes. He sacrificed himself. Not for Lucifer and his bunch of fools, but for *you*, Sir. He didn't *have* to be there at that point in time. He didn't *have* to help me in any way at all. But he *chose* to do what he did. He made the decision on which side of the fence to stand when the end came."

Nodded in agreement as he dismissed the coffee cup from his hand, God blinked both eyes once, and a smile crossed his face. Gabriel was about to continue when a voice behind him stopped him dead in his tracks.

"Hey dude! How's it hanging? Oh, sorry, I forgot, you don't have one to hang, do you? And where's the other? You know, your *He*. I thought I was supposed to ..." A puzzled expression crossed the boy's face, "you know, deliver your message. Wait a minute, what are *you* doing here?"

Standing up quickly, Gabriel checked the smile that threatened to erupt on his face as he turned round and faced the spotty, greasy-haired youth (now clad in skater shorts, dirty trainers, baseball hat and a hooded top bearing the words 'Death's A Bitch ... Just Don't Tell His Wife').

"Well, look what the proverbial cat's dragged in!" Letting the smile win, Gabriel let the now struggling dog drop to the floor and watched as it ran over to the teenager and jumped straight into his thin arms. "It's a long story, Embram, a very long story."

Hugging the animal, Embram skater boy looked at

the angel and then at the occupant of the second chair, his spotty face reddening as he realised who it was.

"Is that *Him?*" he said, keeping the angel between himself and the other, leaning only his head and neck around Gabriel in an attempt to see but not to be seen. "Is he your *He,* Gabe? It is, isn't it? That's your main dude to beat all main dudes, isn't it?"

Sighing, Archangel Gabriel placed both hands on the youth's shoulders and turned him to face the other chair. When its occupant spoke, Embram felt all of his teenage bravado run and hide.

"So *you* are Embram Ferret Frightener, are you? One of Hell's foul demons, who, on a whim, decided to feed the head of my main cherub to his pet!"

Embram felt his face draining of colour as the man in the strange uniform stood up and moved towards him. He felt physically sick when the man stood looking down at him.

"You are the creature who had the *audacity,* the *nerve,* to think itself capable of carrying out a task given directly to one of my Archangels!"

As the man bent down level with his face, Embram closed his eyes and waited again for the oblivion that was long overdue.

"Well, Embram, I'm going to do something a God rarely does himself! I'm saying thank you, Embram Ferret Frightener. Thank you, and please accept this gift from me and a *very* grateful realm of mortal souls."

Embram's eyes snapped open as a full set of feathered angel wings sprouted from between his narrow shoulders, his skater clothing changing into a full (if not a little small) set of angelic armour. Looking down at his friend, Gabriel nodded in approval.

"Nice, gargoyle, very nice! Maybe *now* we can dispense with the words 'dude', 'punk', 'babe' and 'main man'?"

Looking at his reflection in a nearby mirror, Angel

Embram (Third Class) smiled and looked back at the captain, who was still watching him.

"What can I say? It's more than I could ever have imagined in twenty millennia, or even in a hundred millennia! But ..."

"But, Embram? There's a but in this?" (OK, go on then. I know you've been waiting to bring a smutty joke into a dramatic part of the story! Let's have all the 'butt' jokes now, shall we?)

Looking down at the floor and shuffling his booted feet, Angel Embram said quietly, "I want to stay looking like I was ... if that's OK."

It was Gabriel who spoke, the surprise he was feeling showing in his voice. "You want to do what, Embram? You want to stay a spotty little boy riding on a plank of wood with wheels?"

"Are you sure, Embram? Are you positive that's what you want?" Stroking the poodle, Gerald Oliver Davies wore a bemused expression on his face as he waited for the reply.

"Yes, I'm sure. I like it here on this side. No one expects too much of you, and I like the clothes."

Not bothering to hide the surprise that was clearly showing on his face, Mr. Davies rubbed his chin and spoke again. "You understand that *if* you stay here, it will have to be as a mortal. Think hard, Embram! This offer is the *only one* I'm going to make."

Looking at Gabriel, Embram winked and laughed aloud.

"Yes, I'm sure. After all, who would want to spend an eternity looking like a miniature Gabriel?"

Blinking twice, Gerald took Gabriel's arm and led him through the shop, passing shelves full of skateboards and skateboarding accessories as they made their way to the door. Stopping for a moment, Gabriel leaned over and whispered something to the older man. With a sigh Gerald Oliver Davies nodded, smiled, and carried on walking. Looking back and smiling at skater boy Embram and his blue-rinse poodle, Gabriel blinked, and grinned in satisfaction at the new wording that appeared on his friend's hooded top: 'Skaters, Trekkies and Cool Dudes.'

"Look after the soul, Embram, it's the only one you have!" Letting his smile grow, Gabriel turned and left the shop, speaking over his shoulder without looking back. "See you later, skater boy."

"See you soon, cool dude!"

The street was deserted as they walked away from the shop and into the darkness of the late afternoon. An old man in white robes and an angel, side by side, deep in conversation, as they slowly faded from view.

"There is *something* else we need to discuss, Gabriel. It's about this application for a gun licence you've submitted ... And what exactly *is* an M16?"

To be continued ...

Printed in the United Kingdom
by Lightning Source UK Ltd.
122092UK00001B/67-99/A